小樹系列

Little Trees

小樹系列

Little Trees

深夜微光

MIDNIGHT CHANNEL FOR TEENAGERS

App的奇幻世界

作者序

社群媒體中的真假人生

Kelly Kuo

感覺才不久前……。

我離開了台灣，離開這個我向來稱之為「家」的地方。成長過程中，我常覺得自己像個融不進主流的旁觀者。我和大家「不一樣」。我老覺得自己格格不入，難以投入與適應。對我身邊的同儕與老師而言，我的存在可有可無，我甚至感覺他們有意無意忽略我，或對我的想法不以為然。

當時我認為這地方欠缺眼光獨到的人，盡是膚淺之輩……。我需要一個懂得發現我內在真實潛力與特質的地方，當我偶爾不經意犯錯時，我不會因此而被批判攻擊。

我需要另闢天地，在那裡，我的與眾不同，被珍視，也被賞識。

在美國生活的那幾年，我漸漸明白，其實，人人生而平等，不管他所在之處是太平洋上某個不知名小島，或是一個擁有五十個多元文化與社會習俗的廣袤大地上。沒有任何地方會看見誰的獨特潛力。但我倒是領會一件事：我其實並沒有想像中那麼與眾不同。原來，我長久以來的掙扎，並非身邊的人是否懂得欣賞我，而是我不懂得如何以他們能理解的方式來表達自己，進而讓他們認同與賞識我的想法。歷經數年的辛苦耕耘、摸索與學習，掌握新語言的同時，我也學會以新的方式與他人互動，我終於找到指引我日常生活的好原則與提示——只要你不放棄嘗試，人生沒有所謂失敗。

我經常回頭反省這段成長的歲月，並以此來檢視今天的青少年處境。現代青少年幾乎人人擁抱自己的出口——社群媒體。臉書上只有讓你按「讚」的按鈕——沒有讓你表達「討厭」或「反對」的選項。一如「國王的新衣」——當你陶醉於誇大不實的讚譽中太久，你終將失去判斷虛實的能力與發現真相的勇氣。很多時候，你當下所置身的處境，說穿了，根本就是一絲不掛、赤身裸體。

例如：

社群媒體貼文：我之所以在校表現不佳、成績不好，是因為我媽老是在喝酒，害我很難專注學習。

真相：貼文者根本並未在家做功課，她媽媽通常很晚下班，分身乏術，所以無法督責她的學校功課。

社群媒體貼文：我上不了大學是因為我爸爸粗鄙又斤斤計較，他不肯幫我付大學學費。

真相：貼文者根本落榜，沒被任何大學錄取。

社群媒體貼文：為什麼我在學校默默無聞，人氣不足？那是因為我家世背景不夠有錢、不夠顯赫，而且我又長得胖。

真相：貼文者從來不想參與任何學校活動或計畫。

國王新衣的故事結局，就在一個孩子的童言無忌中，直指國王身上根本沒穿衣服，而一語道破虛謊，窘境才落幕。孩子單純不偽裝，有話直說，不擅於掩蓋或扭曲真相。我真希望多一些社群媒體也能以此心態，來引導我們的青少年——帶他們探究，何為事實，不論真相是美好或醜陋，學會欣賞真相的本質；讓他們明白，要在真實世界活出自信，其實需要再努力一點；指引他們發現，原來關懷他人，自己也受惠，這是人生大智慧，也是享樂。

僅以這本書，送給這世上所有青少年的父母。勉勵父母們不斷地竭盡所能，一起想方設法帶領孩子穿越社群媒體刻意修飾與隱瞞的美好假象，去探究真實人生中，原來存在一片如此通透自在的美麗「心」世界。

第一章
CHAPTER 1

突來的應用程式
The App

The stage is illuminated with glaring spotlights. The air inside the auditorium is dark, yet hot and humid, laced with excitement and anticipation. The annual high school marching band audition is a must-see event for all students and teachers alike. The crowd hushes as the speaker makes a crackling sound.

"Next performer, Billie Lin, come up to the stage!"

Billie stands up nervously in front of an auditorium full of students and walks towards the stage. Her hands are sweaty, and her heart is beating at triple speed. The stage lights are glaring in her eyes, and she can't stop sweating from both the heat from the light and her nerves. She can feel her shirt drenched in sweat, stuck to her back, as she stands in the middle of the stage. Dead silence in the auditorium, as if everybody's holding their breath to listen to the audition. She picks up her saxophone, and holds it close to her lips. Her hands tremble a little. What's the first note.... Where should I put my fingers....

The speaker crackles with a piercing feedback pitch, followed by a loud announcement: "Billie Lin, you need to announce your song choice. Points off." Billie's heart just skips a beat hearing Mrs. Hans' stern reminder about the rules of audition.

學校禮堂裡，萬頭攢動，人聲鼎沸。舞台上燈光耀眼，一年一度的校內樂團選拔試奏會開始了。躍躍欲試的選手，與翹首企足的群眾，把現場氛圍搞得熱烈又緊張。

「下一位演出者，林比莉，請上台！」

林比莉在座無虛席的群眾中，羞怯地站起來，走向舞台。她手掌心出汗，心跳加速。舞台的強烈聚光燈，照得她幾乎睜不開眼，加上緊張忐忑，比莉開始冒汗，汗珠大滴小滴落一身。當她終於站在台上時，早已汗流浹背的她，感覺連衣服都快被汗水浸透了。禮堂裡原來的喧鬧，倏忽一片沉寂，靜得出奇；大家屏氣凝神，等著聽她演奏。比莉拿出薩克斯風，把樂器湊近自己的雙唇。比莉的雙手微微顫抖，頭腦一片空白。啊，第一個音是什麼……我的手指該往哪裡擺……。

音響突然傳來刺耳的回音，隨即一段廣播，如雷貫耳地將她喚回現實：「林比莉，妳得先報告妳選的曲目哦！扣分。」當比莉聽到漢斯教練嚴肅地提醒她有關試奏會的規則，心跳頓時漏了一拍。

比莉走到麥克風前。「嗯，抱歉。我是薩克斯風獨奏，曲目是《身體與靈魂，降D大調》。」

好了，我該冷靜下來，拜託，我已經練了成千上萬次了。比莉大口深呼吸，閉上眼睛讓自己聚精會神，把手指

Billie walks up to the microphone. "Um sorry. Saxophone solo from Body and Soul, in D flat major."

OK, I gotta calm down, I've played this song gazillion times. Billie takes a deep breath, closes her eyes to focus, places her fingers on the D keys, slowly blows into the mouthpiece. So far so good, she plays the first few notes. Her palms are still clammy, but her muscle memory is perfectly intact, and her fingers knew exactly where they need to be. Her heartbeat slows down to the rhythm of the melody, her saxophone tones are groovy, and she is feeling the moment. This is her father's favorite song. "It's slow, romantic and soulful, a perfect melody for a peaceful full moon," her father's words lingers in her head. "You need to be lovingly gentle but firm on the mouthpiece, like leading your partner in a slow dance." Her father used to tell her. She applies a gentle push on her cheek to make the saxophone resonate quietly like the moonlight at midnight. Billie is finally confident enough to slowly open her eyes. Her eyes adjust to the spotlights on the stage, and she can see the auditorium now. A packed full house for the school band audition.

That's when it happens.

擺好在D大調的位置上，緩緩地吹出音符。剛開始的幾個曲調，吹得還不錯。雖然手心因汗水而濕潤，但絲毫不影響她的表現，她對自己的手指完全駕馭自如，游刃有餘。她急促的心跳慢慢緩和下來，跟上了音符的節奏，她吹出的曲調悠揚，連自己也陶醉在音樂中。這是她爸爸最愛的曲目，爸爸的評論仍縈繞腦中，揮之不去——「這首曲子和緩、浪漫而深情，最適合平靜祥和的月圓之夜聆聽。」爸爸常常提醒她：「妳在吹這首曲子時，要溫柔而堅定，就像在慢舞中不疾不徐地引導妳的舞伴。」她雙頰稍微使力，讓薩克斯風的共鳴更圓潤飽滿，就像暗夜裡的月光。比莉越來越有自信了，她慢慢睜開雙眼，把視線與舞台上的聚光燈對焦，現在，她終於可以比較輕鬆自在地環顧四周。整個禮堂人滿為患，大夥兒都是為了學校樂團的試奏發表而來。

話說當下，有事發生了。

誰搞砸了這一切？

一切始於眼前這兩個討厭的女生：艾碧愷與柯特琳。她們簡直是學校裡有錢有勢的惡勢力，把比莉的人生搞得痛苦不堪。全校女生都把這兩個恃寵而驕、瘦得像紙片的惡女奉為偶像，而男生則對她們仰慕得五體投地。這兩個

Who Is Screwing Up?

Abigail and Catelyn. The skinny rich bitches of the school, who make her life utterly miserable. Girls idolize them, boys worship them. They command total attention of the entire school body. They hold the power to being popular at school, and they also hold the power to designate the unpopular ones.

Abigail and Catelyn are sitting in the front row of the auditorium. They watch Billie for a while, smiling and giggling, and then Catelyn whispers into Abigail's ears. Abigail nods and gives her approval. Then they both stand up and leave the auditorium. That distracts Billie immensely.... What is that all about? Are they laughing at me? Did I screw up the last note? What's my next note?.... "SQEEEEAAK!" Billie just misplaces her finger on the saxophone and it squeaks. She tries to correct it, with her fingers all over the saxophone, "SQUEAK! SQUEAK!" and now she can't stop squeaking all of her notes. Completely horrified, Billie tries to remember the rest of the song. "SQUEEEAAAK!!!" Unfortunately the only sound coming out of her saxophone is continuous squeaks at this point, no matter what note she tries to play. The whole auditorium starts with quiet giggles and roars into laughter. Billie is totally embarrassed, her face

惡婆娘在校內簡直呼風喚雨，是全校矚目的焦點人物，凡事她們說了算，所以，有些邊緣分子都不得不忍受她們的頤指氣使，甚至飽受她們欺凌與排擠。

當比莉在台上試奏時，艾碧愷與柯特琳就坐在禮堂的前排。她們專注盯著比莉看一會兒，笑得咯咯作響，然後，柯特琳在艾碧愷耳邊竊竊私語，只見艾碧愷點頭示意。然後，兩人起身，離開禮堂。不知為何，她們的舉動大大影響並分散了比莉的專注力，她忍不住暗自心想，怎麼了？那是怎麼一回事？她們是在嘲笑我嗎？哎喲，我剛剛是不是把最後一個音搞砸了？我按錯了嗎？糟糕，我下一個音是什麼啊？……「吱……！」比莉的指法錯置，薩克斯風發出刺耳吱聲。她嘗試糾正，試圖把所有手指都放在薩克斯風上，但無論她怎麼按，樂器仍不停地發出「嘎吱嘎吱」聲。面對這樣的窘境，比莉慌亂無措，她竭盡所能去記起接下來整首曲目的音樂。「吱吱……！」糟糕！又是這個搞砸了的聲音！無論比莉怎麼吹，最終從薩克斯風釋放出來的只剩令人崩潰的聲音。禮堂的群眾開始有些騷動，從竊笑到哄堂大笑。比莉尷尬得無地自容，滿臉羞紅，上衣的裡裡外外都是汗。她試著讓自己冷靜下來，重新掌握之前吹奏時的感覺，但眾人此起彼落的訕笑令她洩氣，一切努力，都是徒勞。

is red hot and her shirt is completely drenched in sweat, back and forth, again. Her effort to try to calm down to get back into the song is futile with the whole auditorium laughing.

"QUIET EVERYBODY!" Mrs. Hans yells over the speaker. "Billie Lin, it doesn't seem like you have practiced enough for this audition. You may leave the stage now."

Billie grips tightly on the saxophone and runs off the stage, holding back her tears until she got outside of the auditorium. I've never had talent, I don't belong in the band. Now everybody's going to be laughing at me.... Who cares? Who cares about playing in the band? It's a lame hobby anyway. It is totally lame. Everything is lame. My life sucks.

Her phone beeps. "Wanna walk home together?" It is a text from Tianna, Billie's best friend. Billie takes a long sigh, wipes off her tears, ignores Tianna's message and walks home by herself.

Nobody's home, as usual. Good, she wants to be left alone for the rest of her life anyway. Billie heats up a leftover pizza in the microwave and scrolls through her social media feeds. "Congratulations to Catelyn made it in the school band!" A new tweet from Abigail. Catelyn

「大家安靜！」漢斯教練透過麥克風大聲制止。「林比莉，我看妳對這場試奏會的練習很不足哦。妳現在可以下去了。」

比莉緊抓著薩克斯風，快速跑離舞台，她忍住奪眶而出的淚水，頭也不回地一路跑到禮堂外，才發洩心中自暴自棄的挫敗情緒：「反正我永遠也不會有什麼才能啦，我根本不屬於什麼樂團。這下嗝屁了，大家都可以拿我當笑柄了……算了，沒什麼了不起的！管他咧！誰在乎參加樂團啊？反正也只是個無聊的興趣！無聊蹩腳，徹底無趣！什麼狗屎人生，討厭！」

比莉的電話響了幾聲。「想要一起走路回家嗎？」比莉打開手機簡訊，那是閨蜜恬娜傳來的訊息。比莉嘆了一口氣，拭去臉上淚水，對恬娜的簡訊置之不理，獨自走路回家。

一如以往，家裡空無一人。比莉心想，隨便啦，反正，接下來的這輩子都一個人過日子好了，沒差！比莉把隔夜的披薩放進微波爐熱一熱，滑開手機，開始瀏覽她的社群媒體。艾碧愷剛剛在動態消息上，貼上了一則最新消息：「恭喜柯特琳成功被樂團錄取！」柯特琳進入樂團？憑她？那個皮包骨的紙片惡女，肯定是賄賂漢斯教練才進得了樂團。還好我沒在樂團裡，誰想要和那兩個噁心的女

made it in the band? Ugh those skinny bitches, I bet they bribed Mrs. Hans to be in the band. Good thing I'm not in the band, who wants to hang with those two? I am a nobody, living in this crappy apartment, mom and dad are never around and I pretty much grew up all by myself.

She hears unlocking of the front door, her mom peeps her head in the door. "Oh hi Billie! My little sweetie pie! You're here!" Her mother stumbles into the apartment, tripping over her own feet. She has a silly smile smeared on her face, and smells of alcohol. "Of course I'm here mom, I live here." Billie replies coldly. "Oh you are a funny kid." Billie's mother reaches over to the fridge door and gets herself a beer. What, another one? She gets drunk every night after work, and continues to drink at home. Pathetic. Billie rolls her eyes, walks back to her room and slammed the door shut. "Billie! You ungrateful thing! Is this how you talk to your mother? I worked two jobs to raise you because your father never gives us money, and what do I get from you? Absolutely NOTHING, not even a THANK YOU!" Her mother yells outside of Billie's room. Again, more evidence that my life sucks and nobody cares about me and I am better left alone.

生在樂團裡？比莉開始自我怨懟；唉，我是個無名小卒，住在毫不起眼的公寓裡，爸媽從來都不在家，我好像就這麼一個人長大的。

比莉聽見有人打開前門，媽媽從門縫探頭進來。「哦，比莉！我的小可愛！妳在家啊！」媽媽跌跌撞撞地踏入家門，一個重心不穩，差點把自己給絆倒了。媽媽臉上掛著醉茫茫的笑意，一股酒精的味道，四溢屋內。「我當然在啊，媽，我住這裡哦。」比莉漠然回應。「啊，妳真是個有趣的孩子。」媽媽每晚工作後都喝得醉醺醺，回到家以後再繼續喝。悲哀。比莉翻了個白眼，無奈走回自己的臥室，用力甩門。「比莉！妳這個忘恩負義的傢伙！這是妳跟妳媽講話的態度嗎？欸，妳知道我得兼兩份工作來養活妳嗎？妳爸爸從來就沒拿錢回來，我這麼辛苦持家到底從妳這裡得到什麼？我什麼都沒有！妳連一聲謝謝都沒有！」媽媽在比莉房門外抓狂嘶吼。比莉暗自思忖，唉，再一次證明我的人生一塌糊塗，根本沒人在乎我！我看我還是被孤立比較好吧。

「叮！」比莉的手機螢幕亮了一下。或許是恬娜的第二封簡訊。比莉把手機拿過來看。咦，是個不具名的門號傳來的訊息，內容寫道：「您是否覺得自己被錯待、人生不公平？您的社交生活因為身邊的惡人而讓自己痛苦不

"Ding!" Her phone lights up. Probably another text from Tianna. Billie picks up her phone. It is a message from an unknown caller: 'Do you feel like you're unfairly treated in life? Is your social life in a state of misery because of very bad people around you? We have a new social platform that is designed to expose them! Don't let them ruin your life anymore, join the movement! Click this link.' As if... this app is designed for me, my life is miserable because of everybody else! It's about time that something good happens to me. Enough about the skinny bitches in the world and drunk parents, an app for REAL people, like me. Yaaas please. Billie clicks on the link.

The Unusual Midnight Moment

"Ta-da-li-la-la~~~" An electronic space age music plays loudly on her phone, followed by numerous fireworks on the screen, and an icon spins into the screen on her cell phone. "Midnight Moment", it says, in a bright neon purple and yellow colored font. An overly enthusiastically dancing animation, kind of shaped like a star with arms and legs, greets Billie on the screen. "Hi there Billie Lin! Welcome to Midnight Moment. I'm Starr, I am your personal guide."

堪？我們為您提供一個全新的社群平台來揭發這一切真相！不要再被這些狗屁倒灶的事，毀了您的人生，請點選以下連結，加入我們的行動！」這個應用程式怎麼看都像是為我量身定制的呢！說得多麼貼切，我的人生就是因為其他人的錯，而被搞得慘不忍睹！該是來點鴻運好事的時候了。我實在受夠了這世上的紙片惡女和醉茫茫的母親。啊，這個適時出現的應用程式，就是給我這種「真正需要」的人使用的。好得不得了！我迫不及待。比莉隨即按了上面顯示的連結。

不尋常的深夜與微光

「噠—啦—里—啦—啦……」一段嘹亮的電子音樂，在她手機上響起，螢幕上隨即出現此起彼落的絢爛煙火，接著是一段閃爍著霓虹亮紫與黃色字體的標誌，在螢幕上閃過——「深夜微光」。一個類似配上雙手與雙腳的星狀動畫，以熱情奔放的酷炫舞蹈，在螢幕上問候比莉。「嗨！林比莉！歡迎加入『深夜微光』的行列，我是星兒，我是妳的個人導師。」

「讓我來解釋妳可以如何使用這個應用程式。其實很簡單，妳只需要在下方白色框框裡寫下妳的貼文，內容可以是別人如何對待妳的種種行徑，或這整個制度是如何虛

"Let me explain how this app works. It's very simple, you just write your post in this white box below. It could be what others did to you. Or how the system is rigged. That's it. We use the most advanced AI, short for Artificial Intelligence technology, to transcribe your written post into a video. Your video will be ready after midnight. Can I emphasize again you are the very few selected people to pioneer the future of social app? Try it now!" Starr points to a white text box on her phone. Billie thought for a second. This will be a good platform tell the real story for the real people. I'm going to reveal how the privileged students like Abigail and Catelyn causes injustice to the common people like us at school. So she types away on the little white box:

"May 29th, 2019. Mr. Frank let us go to lunch early, so I sat at our usual corner table in the cafeteria, waiting for Tianna. Abigail and Catelyn came by. Catelyn yelled at me for no reason, claiming that this was 'their' table, and shooed me to go sit somewhere else. Abigail laughed and said that I was too fat to sit there. Conner Sutherland walked by and joined them in the laughing match. I had to run away because I was not welcomed at all here. This school is run by bunch of selfish, privileged people." Billie reads it one more time, smiles and clicks

假不義。就這麼簡單。我們用最先進的人工智慧科技，把妳所寫的內容改編成動態影音。這段專屬於妳的動態影片，就會在天亮之前，準時完工。請容我再強調一次，妳是少數被選上成為我們社群軟體的先驅者！別遲疑，現在就試試看！」星兒指向比莉手機裡出現的一個白色框框，示意她把貼文內容寫於此。思索片刻之後，比莉想，這真是個揭露真相的好平台。嗯，我來揭發像艾碧愷與柯特琳這些既得利益者的真面目，把她們的惡形惡狀都公諸於世，看看她們如何讓我們這群學校裡的「平民百姓」感覺差人一等，真是不公不義！於是，比莉開始在空格裡大書特書：

「2019年5月29日。法蘭克老師讓我們提早下課去吃午餐。和往常一樣，我坐在餐廳熟悉的角落等恬娜過來。艾碧愷與柯特琳走進餐廳。柯特琳沒來由地朝著我大吼，聲稱這是『她們的』餐桌，把我趕到其他地方。艾碧愷在一旁大笑，還一邊調侃我太胖了，那個位子容納不了我。康納經過時，也加入欺壓陣營，跟著大夥兒嘲笑我。我不得不逃往他處，因為我完全被他們排擠。這間學校根本任由一群自私自利、占盡優勢的人為所欲為。」比莉寫好這段文字後，重新讀一次，臉上帶著笑意，點選「寄出貼文」。星兒返回螢幕。「第一份貼文完成了，很棒哦！我

on "submit post". Starr comes back on the screen. "Good job on your first post! We'll work on it right away, your video will be done by midnight. In the meantime, let us show you a sample video posted by other users on the platform." A small video screen shows up and starts playing.

The video zooms into a boy, walking by himself with a basketball in his hand. Billie recognizes the boy. Ah, isn't that Cameron King , the co-captain of the school basketball team? A couple of gangsters looking kids show up and block his path. OMG, that is the infamous bully duo in school. The taller kid walked up to Cameron. "Well well well, isn't it our favorite basketball star? Did you bring the money?" Cameron looked around to see if there was anybody around. "I told you that I'll have it by end of the next week. Why are you here? That's not our agreement." There was a slight tremble in Cameron's voice, he was outnumbered but was trying to hold his ground. The shorter kid walked up. "Well, we need money now. We figured something so important, I'm sure you don't mind paying up sooner. So do you have it? Or, should we start leaking our little secret? Hehe." Cameron frowned and lowered his voice: "Fine. I don't have it today but I will have it by end of the week. Same

們立即為妳編輯製作，趕在天亮前完工。與此同時，讓我們秀一段其他人使用這個平台貼文以及我們製作的影片讓妳看看。」一段影片隨即在螢幕中出現。

影片上的鏡頭拉近，那是一個男孩，手裡拿著籃球，獨自走在路上。啊！比莉認識那個男生，他不就是卡麥龍嗎？學校籃球校隊副隊長嘛！忽然，出現了兩個看似流氓的男生擋住他的去路。哦！天啊！那是學校裡惡名昭彰的混混雙人組。其中一個高個兒走到卡麥龍面前。「哎喲，瞧瞧，這不就是我們大名鼎鼎的籃球明星嗎！有沒有把錢帶來？」卡麥龍四處張望，確定是否有其他人在附近。「我已經跟你說了，下禮拜前才會準備好，你怎麼會出現在這裡？這不是我們之前說好的協定哦。」卡麥龍的聲音有些顫抖，雖然他寡不敵眾，但還是努力表達立場。比較矮的另一個傢伙走上前。「我們現在就需要錢。我們發現了一些很重要的東西，我相信你一定不介意提早把錢給我們。你到底身上有沒有錢？不然的話，我們就把新發現的小祕密公布出來囉？嘻嘻！」卡麥龍蹙眉惱怒，壓低聲量說：「隨便你。我今天身上沒錢，但我會在下週前準備好。同樣的時間和地點。還有，不要在校園裡跟我講話，那是我們已經說好的。」

兩個流氓屁孩詭計得逞，仰頭笑著離開。「那就週

time, same place. Don't ever talk to me in school, that's our agreement."

The two bullies laughed and walked away. "See ya Friday!" The video zooms into Cameron's frowning face then ends. Billie is quite shocked.... Wow Cameron King, the ever-so-confident-borderline-egotistic Cameron King, in a completely different shade of light and being blackmailed by the bully duo. I wonder what's going on.

Right when she is still pondering about that video, the app closes itself, and also disappears from her phone screen. "Wait, I want to watch that video again!" Billie quickly scrolls through her phone but in vain, the app is nowhere to be found on her phone. What happens to the app? Is it some type of fluke? Billie gives up the search and goes to bed.

Billie has some really weird dreams that night. She dreams of her saxophone all bent and rusted, squeaking note after note while a loud laughter roars in the background. She turns around to see who is laughing, it is her mother, holding her hands, half drunk and slurring "I'm not drunk honey, I'm just trying to relax...." As soon as she lets go of her mother's hands, a sad Cameron holds her feet and cries: "I don't have the money today.... I don't have the money today...." Then

五見囉！」鏡頭聚焦於卡麥龍緊鎖的眉頭與苦臉，鏡頭停格，結束。比莉心頭一震……哇！卡麥龍欸！我印象中那個超級傲慢又趾高氣揚的卡麥龍，在影片裡卻光輝盡失，垂頭喪氣，還任由兩個流氓小混混脅迫討錢。我太好奇了，這到底是怎麼一回事？

比莉困惑不已，陷入深思，眼前的應用程式倏地自行關閉，也從手機螢幕上消失。「等等，我還想再看一次！」比莉趕緊滑開手機，但怎麼試也沒辦法，應用程式就這麼從手機裡銷聲匿跡。這應用程式到底是怎麼一回事啊？該不會是幸運中了什麼獎吧？比莉遍尋不著這個程式，只好作罷，上床睡覺。

那一晚，比莉做了幾個很奇怪的夢。她夢見自己的薩克斯風被折得歪七扭八，腐蝕生鏽，還發出一個又一個吱吱作響的雜音，背後傳來陣陣高調刺耳的笑聲。她轉身環顧四周，想看看是誰在笑，哦，竟是她媽媽。媽媽抓著比莉的手，半醉半醒地含糊嘟噥：「寶貝我沒有喝醉，我只是想讓自己放輕鬆……」正當她把媽媽的手甩開時，神情落寞的卡麥龍卻跑出來緊抓她的雙腳，哭著哀求她：「我今天沒錢……我今天沒錢……」。然後，她被扔到一片漆黑的空間裡，比莉的身體不斷旋轉搖擺，忽然，星兒出現了，帶著一貫的愉悅聲調，與她一起在黑暗中舞動旋轉。

she is tossed into a deep darkness, swirling and turning and Starr shows up, swirling with her in the darkness with the usual cheerful tone. "Our AI is doing our best to produce your post! There is a lot of interpretation from your story, but with our awesome technology the video will be very close to the truth! We're going to learn so much about each other in this process, it's so exciting!" Starr's voice echoes in the deep darkness as Billie swirls faster and deeper into the far end of the darkness.

Billie wakes up in the morning with a cold sweat. Her sheet is all wet from the sweat. Wow that was some weird dream. "Ding!" She reaches for her phone and Starr pops up on the screen.

"Congratulations! Your first post is up!" Starr says in a cheerful voice. Ah, so the app still exists! She clicks on the "watch my video" button.

Video pans to her English class teacher, Mr. Frank. This was from her class yesterday. "Class, if you finished your assignment, you may break for lunch. For those who didn't, I'm going to give you the next 25 minutes to finish it up." Billie packed up her bag and stood up, ready to leave the classroom. Selina pulled her arm and whispered: "Billie you can't leave, we didn't finish our assignment. You gotta stay and finish it." Billie whispered

「我們的人工智慧正竭盡所能在製作妳的貼文！妳的故事有好多要詮釋的情節，但以我們高超的科技智慧來處理，妳放心好了，妳的影片一定會非常接近事實！這過程也讓大家可以更互相了解，真的太興奮了！」比莉的身軀越轉越快，彷彿沒入黑暗的盡頭，而星兒的聲音則在幽微暗處迴響。

早晨醒來的剎那，比莉冒了一身冷汗。她的被單都是汗水。哇！那真是離奇又怪異的夢境。「叮」！她拿起手機一看，星兒出現螢幕上。

「恭喜妳！妳的第一則貼文已上傳！」星兒開心宣告。啊，所以那應用程式還存在！比莉立即點開「觀賞我的影片」按鍵。

影片開始播放。鏡頭對準比莉的英文老師，法蘭克老師。那是昨天上課的情境。「同學們，你們如果完成功課了，可以先自己下課去吃午餐。那些還沒做完的同學，我再給你們二十五分鐘去完成。」比莉收拾包包，起身準備離開教室。薛麗娜推一下她的手肘，在她耳邊低語：「比莉妳不可以先走，我們還沒把功課做完；妳得留下來完成。」比莉低聲回應：「妳就幫幫忙順便做兩份嘛！感激不盡哦。」她給薛麗娜一個詭異神祕的笑容，然後，轉身從容離開教室。薛麗娜沮喪又無可奈何。鏡頭一路緊跟著

back:" Can't you do it for both of us? Thanks a bunch." She slyly smiled at Selina as she headed out of the classroom. Selina was visibly upset. The video followed Billie to the cafeteria. She headed for the corner table. Abigail and Catelyn were sitting at the corner table, chatting away. Billie hesitated, she looked at the table and the two girls awkwardly. Abigail saw Billie looking their way. "I'm guessing that you want this table?" She said coldly to Billie. Catelyn chimed in, "You and your friend always take this table. What's so great about this table?" Abigail stood up. "C'mon, we're done here anyway. Here, you can have your favorite table back." Billie's face turned red and murmured, "Who... who wants that table! You can keep your damn table." she turned and walked away as fast as she can. At the exit of the cafeteria, Conner Sutherland walked by Billie. "What's up Billie?" He smiled as he walked by, but Billie ignored Conner and walked away. The video ends.

What Makes A Fact Fact?

Billie is horrified as her face turned blue.... How did this "AI" know about Mr. Frank, Selina and the assignment? How did it know about the conversation with Abigail and Catelyn? And ok, maybe Conner wasn't

比莉到餐廳。她走向餐廳角落那張桌子。艾碧愷與柯特琳剛好占用了那張桌子，兩人坐在那兒聊天。比莉有些遲疑，她看著那張桌子和旁邊的兩個女孩，顯然神情有些不自在。艾碧愷看見比莉的視線往她們的方向投來，於是她漠然詢問比莉：「我猜，妳想要坐這裡，對吧？」柯特琳插話說道：「妳和妳的朋友老愛用這張桌子。這桌子是有什麼特別神奇的魔力嗎？」艾碧愷站起來，說道：「走吧，反正我們也不用了。吶，給妳，妳可以擁有妳最愛的桌子了。」比莉尷尬得滿臉通紅，嘴裡嘀咕：「誰啊……誰要這張桌子啊！這張臭桌子妳留著自己用吧！」她轉身，以最快的步伐盡速走開。在餐廳出口處，康納迎面走來，與比莉擦身而過。「嘿，比莉，還好嗎？」他邊走邊微笑向比莉打招呼，但比莉對康納的問候視而不見，逕自走開。這段影片就停在這裡。

誰的真相？

比莉看得膽戰心驚，面色鐵青……這個「人工智慧」怎麼知道法蘭克老師、薛麗娜和那些功課的事啊？它又怎麼會對我和艾碧愷、柯特琳三人之間的對話內容瞭若指掌？好吧，或許康納當時不在她們身邊，但他平常真的常和她們兩個女生混在一起啊，我合理猜想康納應該也會加

there when this happened. But he hangs with them all the time, he probably was laughing at me anyway. Nobody can see this video...! "No.... No.... No.... I don't want to post this. Starr...Starr...where are you? Where is the 'delete' button?" Billie frantically clicks through all the buttons on the app, attempting to delete the video. Swiftly, Starr shows up on the screen. "I hope you enjoyed the first post! Come back later today for more posts!" Billie yells at Starr, "I don't want to post this, you idiot! Delete! Delete!" But Starr disappears and the app closes itself, again. "No, don't disappear! I need to delete this post! Where is that app?" Billie yells and scrolls through her phone searching for the app, but the icon is nowhere to be found. What the heck is this app? Did anybody watch that video? I am DOOMED. Billie puts the phone down, deflated.

Just then, "Billie! Billie! Ready to go? We're almost late for school!" Tianna yells from downstairs. "Coming!" Billie grabs her backpack and rushes for the door.

"What happened, Billie? You look terrible. Your eyes are bloodshot." Tianna asks Billie as they walk together to school. "Oh, it's nothing.... Just didn't sleep well, that's all." Billie lies. Does Tianna know about

入她們的嘲笑大隊嘛。但是，哦不！不能讓任何人看到這段影片……！「不……不……不……我絕對不可以讓這段影片被任何人看到，星兒……星兒……你在哪裡？『刪除』按鍵在哪裡？」比莉發了瘋似的，按遍了應用程式的所有按鍵，想方設法要將這段影片刪除。星兒旋即出現螢幕上，說：「希望妳對首篇貼文的內容感到滿意！稍晚記得回來分享更多精彩貼文！」比莉對著星兒怒吼：「你這個大白癡，我不要你放上這些影片！刪掉刪掉！」話一說完，星兒瞬間消失，應用程式也再度自動關閉。「哦不！不准消失！我需要刪除這些影片！程式跑到哪裡了？」比莉氣急敗壞地大吼大叫，一邊滑著手機尋找相關程式，但那標誌怎麼找也找不到。這到底是什麼應用程式啊？到底有沒有人已經看到那段影片？天啊！我這下身敗名裂了！比莉心灰意冷，把手機放下。

「比莉！比莉！準備出門了嗎？我們快要遲到了啦！」恬娜適時出現，在樓下呼喚。「來了！」比莉一把抓起背包，衝到門口。

「比莉，妳怎麼了？發生什麼事啊？妳看起來不太好。妳的眼球都布滿血絲。」兩人走路上學途中，恬娜關心詢問。「哦，沒什麼……就只是睡得不太好。」比莉輕描淡寫地撒了個謊。咦，恬娜知道這個應用程式嗎？

this app? "Oh, must be the audition that got you all wired up huh. So how did it go? How come you didn't reply to my text yesterday?" Billie is not in the mood to describe her biggest fail at the audition, even to her best friend Tianna. "You know, this band thing is pretty lame anyway, I don't want to be in the band after all. I don't care how it went. Truth." Billie lies, which is her default protection mechanism. Tianna looks puzzled. "I thought you've always wanted to be in the band? What happened...."

"Hey Ti-ti, have you heard of this app...called Midnight Moment?" Billie interrupts Tianna to change subject from the audition. "Midnight what? Never heard. Is it any good?" Oh good, Tianna doesn't have that app. Which means she has not seen the video. "Nah, don't worry about it. Just something I heard."

"Hey guys! Wait up!" Billie turns her head, it's Conner Sutherland running towards them. Oh no, I hope he's not here to talk about what happened at the cafeteria yesterday. Or the audition. Please go away. Billie tries to ignore Conner and continued walking. Tianna's eyes light up with a sweet smile, slows down to chat with Conner, "Hi Conner. Didn't know that you walk to school too. Are you practicing this afternoon?"

「啊，我猜應該是試奏會讓妳整個人精疲力盡哦。所以，昨天狀況怎麼樣？妳昨天怎麼沒有回覆我的留言？」就算對象是閨蜜，比莉也沒有心情敘述昨天在禮堂經歷的那場人生大挫敗。「妳知道的嘛，學校樂團其實蠻無趣的，我根本就不想加入，說實在話，我也不在乎最後結果怎麼樣。」比莉掩飾實情，沒說真話，那是她自我保護的防禦機制。這下，恬娜有些困惑了。「我還以為妳一直很想加入學校樂團欸，不是嗎？到底是怎麼了？」

「嘿，恬恬啊，妳有沒有聽過一個應用程式……叫做『深夜微光』？」比莉打斷恬娜的提問，藉此轉移試奏會的話題。「深夜什麼啊？沒聽過欸。好玩嗎？」呼，太好了，恬娜沒有聽過這個應用程式。那就意味著她沒看過那個影片。「不，不好玩，沒什麼啦，我只是聽說的。」

「嗨，同學！等等我！」比莉回頭一看，原來是康納，他正跑向她們。哦不！我希望他不要提起昨天在學校餐廳的事。還有試奏會的事，我也不想聽。拜託走開。比莉想要擺脫康納，不理他，繼續前行。但身邊的恬娜卻笑臉迎人，放慢腳步回頭與康納攀談起來。「嗨，康納。我還不曉得原來你也走路上學啊。你今天下午會去練球嗎？」

康納是籃球校隊隊長，身高183公分，他臉上的笑容

Conner Sutherland is the captain of the school basketball team. He is 6 feet tall, with a smile that melts any girl. "Oh yeah, the regional championship is coming up so it's practice, practice, practice! I was wondering if you guys are planning on going to the Spring Dance party." Oh yeah.... The Spring Dance party is coming soon. Billie never goes to any of the dance event, for one reason or another. It's another one of those skinny bitches' shows anyway, how lame. Tianna's eyes sparkle even more, "Of course we are going to the Spring Dance party! Are you?" and looks at Conner hopefully. "Well, I was thinking about it, but just wondering if it's worthwhile, you know, with all the practices taking so much time.... But if you guys are going, I'll definitely think about it. All right, I'm gonna take off, see you guys later." Conner dashes over to his basketball team mate on the street. "Ti-ti, you love Conner, don't you? It's sooooo obvious." Billie teases Tianna. Tianna blushes, "Oh, well, I don't know, stop teasing me Billie." Billie is about to tease Tianna some more, when suddenly she sees Cameron King walking by. Billie can't stop staring at Cameron, thinking about the video. I wonder why he is involved with those bullies. Cameron notices Billie staring at him but ignores Billie and walks into school.

足以融化任何女孩。「會呀！區域錦標賽快開打了，所以現在就得練習、練習、再練習！對了，我在想說，不曉得妳們有沒有計畫參加『春天舞會』呢！」對呀……「春天舞會」快到了。因為種種原因，比莉從來沒參加過任何類似的舞會。再說，那是幾個紙片惡女的場子，沒搞頭，無聊！但恬娜可不這麼想。一聽到舞會，恬娜雙眼炯炯發亮，興奮地回答：「『春天舞會』啊！我們當然會去參加！你呢？」恬娜滿懷期待地看著康納。「嗯，我還在考慮，不曉得是不是值得花時間去參加，妳知道的啦，練球實在占據我太多時間了……不過，如果妳們會去，我會認真考慮看看。好吧，我該走了，再見。」康納加快腳步追上路邊一名隊友。「恬恬，妳愛上康納了，對吧？好……明顯哦！」比莉調侃恬娜。恬娜被說得臉紅心跳，「我不知道欸，比莉，別再取笑我啦。」比莉還想要繼續開閨蜜的玩笑，忽然瞥見卡麥龍向她們走來。比莉忍不住盯著卡麥龍看，一邊想起她所看過的影片。我很好奇，卡麥龍怎會和那些流氓混混扯上關係呢？卡麥龍注意到比莉投來的眼光，但假裝沒看到，逕自走進學校。

午休。比莉朝著學校餐廳走去，準備和恬娜會合。頃刻間，比莉還來不及反應，只感覺有人用力抓著她的手臂，把她拉到空無一人的教室裡。「幹嘛啦……哦，是

Lunch break. Billie walks towards the cafeteria to meet up with Tianna. Somebody suddenly grabs her arms and pulls her into an empty classroom. "WHAT THE..... Oh, it's you." Billie is surprised with the move, but even more surprised to see who pulled her. It is Cameron King. "You've seen the video, haven't you?" Cameron looks sternly at Billie. "Um.... What video?" Billie smiles cowardly, tries to deny anything to do with the app. "Don't lie, I can tell from your look. I know you've seen it. Just so you know, I've seen yours, so we're even." WHAAAAAT???? "What do you mean? You have the app? You've seen MY video?" Billie would really love to have a deep black hole where she can hide forever. That is a super embarrassing video and she can pretty much kiss her school social life goodbye. My life is over, somebody has seen my video. Not just anybody, Cameron King, the ultra-egotistic self-centered Cameron King who only cares about himself and his basketball team championship.

Cameron sits down in a chair. "Look, I'm new to that app, I don't know exactly how it works. I watched your video by accident when I was trying to delete my video." Ah, Cameron has the same problem with the app. Billie sits down next to Cameron. "You've seen the video.

你！」突如其來的一陣推拉把比莉嚇了一跳，當她定下神來發現誰在拉扯她時，她更驚詫了。竟然是卡麥龍。「妳看過那個影片了，對嗎？」卡麥龍的眼神犀利，盯著比莉看。比莉心虛地想要閃躲，裝傻笑問：「嗯……什麼影片啊？」她試圖否認所有與那個應用程式相關的提問。「不要騙我，我從妳的表情就知道了。我知道妳看過了。所以妳應該也知道，我也看過妳的影片了，這下可好了，我們扯平。」什麼！你說什麼？「你這是什麼意思啊？你有那個應用程式嗎？你說你看過我的影片？」無地自容的比莉，恨不得有個地洞讓她鑽進去，永遠也不必現身。那簡直是個宇宙無敵難堪的影片，窘到足以讓她從學校的社交生活中永遠消失，永無翻身之日。我這輩子徹底毀了，已經有人看過我的影片了。不是任何一個人，而是卡麥龍，那個超級傲慢又自命不凡的卡麥龍，眼裡只有自己與籃球錦標賽的傢伙。

卡麥龍好整以暇地坐在椅子上。「聽我說，我對這個應用程式一無所知，我根本不曉得怎麼操作。我本來只想刪除我的影片，然後不小心看到妳的那一段影片。」啊，卡麥龍和我一樣，對這應用程式無計可施。比莉坐在卡麥龍旁邊。「你看過了，那或許還有更多人也將看到。我這一生完蛋了！我就知道自己霉運當頭，好事總輪不到

Maybe more people will see it. My life is over. I knew it, nothing good ever happens to me." Billie stutters. Cameron grabs Billie's arms and looks at her seriously. "I can't have my video circulating, I'm the co-captain of the championship basketball team. I'm going to try to delete it somehow. In the meantime, I need you to promise me that you won't tell anybody about the video." Billie is not listening, she is still drowning in her own sorrow and despair and thinking of a way to not come to school anymore, ever. "Billie Lin. I need you to promise me." Cameron yells at Billie to get her attention. Billie looks at Cameron sadly. "My life is over. More people will see my video and it is all over. I knew it. I knew it. Nothing good ever happens to me."

Cameron shakes Billie with both arms. "Look, so far I don't know if anybody else can see our videos. If we act quickly, maybe we can stop other people from seeing it. You need to promise me, otherwise I'm going to tell everybody about your video. I have a LOT more to lose than you, Billie Lin, you are a nobody in school. The person in jeopardy is me, not you. Do we have an agreement?" Billie can't decide if she is offended or comforted with Cameron's statement, she is fuming but also feeling a little more hopeful that Cameron King is

我。」比莉結結巴巴嘟噥著。卡麥龍抓著比莉雙臂，嚴肅地看著她。「我不能讓我的影片四處流傳，我是籃球校隊副隊長。我無論如何會想辦法刪除掉。現在，我需要妳答應我，保守祕密，不可以告訴任何人這段影片。」比莉根本聽而不聞，此時此刻，她自身難保，灰心喪志到彷彿人生走到絕境般，一邊盤算該如何遠走高飛，永遠從學校消失。「林比莉。我需要妳答應我這件事。」卡麥龍朝著比莉喊，想要喚起她的注意力。比莉頹喪地看著卡麥龍。「我的人生已經崩壞了。還有更多人會看到我的影片，一切都完了。我就知道。我就知道。好事總輪不到我。」

卡麥龍以雙手用力搖著比莉，彷彿要把她搖醒：「聽好，直到目前為止，我不曉得是否有其他人看過我們的影片。但如果我們行動快速，或許我們還有機會阻止別人去看。但妳要先答應我，不然的話，我會讓大家都知道妳的影片。妳想過嗎？我要付的代價比妳更多更大欸！林比莉，妳在學校只是無名小卒好嗎！我的名聲那麼高，岌岌可危的人是我，不是妳！好吧，我們是不是達成共識了？」聽卡麥龍的這番話，比莉一時分不清自己到底該生氣或欣慰；她雖然憤憤不平，但又抱持一點希望，但願卡麥龍真的可以解決這個應用程式的問題。比莉長嘆了一口氣：「好吧，答應你。那你一旦找到可以解決的處理方

trying to fix this app. She lets out a long sigh. "OK, deal. You gotta tell me how to delete the video once you figure it out. I'll keep your secret as long as you keep mine." Cameron heads out of the empty classroom, "Good deal. I gotta go. Don't forget out little pact. Miss Squeaky." Miss Squeaky? OK, that's it, I officially hate Cameron King.

法，一定要讓我知道。只要你也守口如瓶，我也會保守你的祕密。」卡麥龍走出那間空蕩蕩的教室之前，對比莉說：「一言為定。我得走了。記得我們的協定哦，嘎吱小姐。」啥？嘎吱小姐？好吧，夠了，從今而後，本人正式宣告——我討厭卡麥龍。

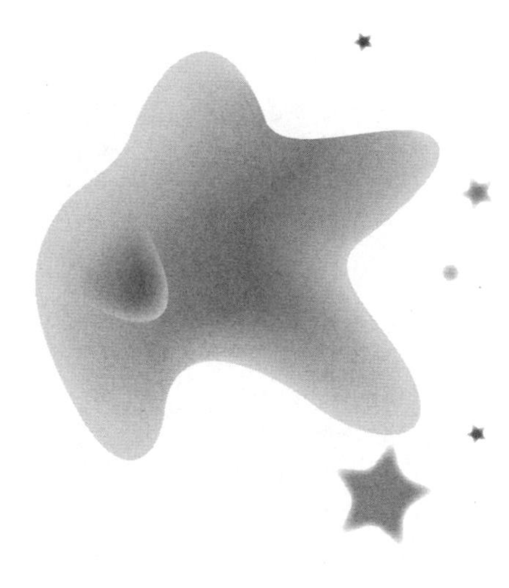

第二章
CHAPTER 2

哪門子的應用程式啊？
What the App?

After school. Tianna can't stop talking with extreme excitement. "...Oh and Mrs. Beverly also said that if this works out, I can also apply for a scholarship to continue with this project in university. Can you believe it, scholarship! My mom would be so happy!" Billie is completely absent minded, thinking about the pact with Cameron. She pulls out her phone, nope, still no Midnight Moment.

"Billie? Are you listening to me? I need your help on this project!" Billie looks up at Tianna. "Oh sorry Titi, What's that again, what do you want me to help?" Tianna is upset with Billie's indifference, but can't hide her excitement. "My proposal for the youth literature program got approved by the school newspaper! They also got PTA to fund the program and recruited bunch of volunteers on the program! I need you to help design a logo and the poster for the program, since you're good at art stuff." Billie doesn't wait to hear the last part of that sentence before she starts screaming.

"PTA? You mean, Abigail's mother, who runs the PTA? Abigail is funding your program? And you still want to do this, although she is the main reason why our life is so miserable? I can't believe you, Tianna! What's next, Abigail is going to be your best friend instead of

放學後。恬娜簡直掩不住內心的激動與興奮，滔滔不絕：「……喔！對了，比佛利老師還說，如果這方法行得通，我也可以同時申請獎學金，未來還可以在大學繼續這個計畫。妳相信嗎？獎學金欸！我媽一定會超高興的！」比莉心神不寧，惦記著與卡麥龍之間的協定，儘管恬娜口若懸河地說個不停，她卻聽而不聞。她把手機拿出來，猛然又想起，喔不，現在還不到「深夜微光」時刻。

「比莉！妳在聽我說話嗎？我這個計畫需要妳的幫忙！」比莉看著恬娜，恍然被拉回現實：「哦，抱歉恬恬，妳剛剛說什麼？可以再說一次嗎？妳需要我幫什麼忙啊？」比莉的敷衍與心不在焉，令恬娜有些悶悶不樂，不過，絲毫無損她的興奮之情，她重申：「我那份青少年文學課程的企劃被期刊錄取了！家長教師協會打算要為這個課程募款，還要招募一群志工來協助這個課程！我需要妳幫我設計一個課程標誌和海報，因為美術方面的專長非妳莫屬了，好嗎？」比莉還沒聽到最後一句便尖聲驚叫。

「妳說啥？家長教師協會？妳是指艾碧愷的媽媽當主席的那個家長教師協會？所以，艾碧愷也會為妳的課程募款？妳明知這個女人把我們的生活搞得多麼灰頭土臉，妳居然還想要繼續這個計畫？我真的無法再相信妳了，恬娜！然後呢？接下來妳是不是要告訴我，艾碧愷會取代

me??" Tianna frowns. "Well, yes, actually Abigail is going to be helping out with the promotion. We need a lot of help for this program. We need you too, Billie." Billie is even more upset. "We? Abigail and you are already a 'we'? She is part of your new world already? Well, sounds like the mighty duo Abigail and Tianna's got plenty of help on your little program, you don't need me. Congratulations on moving up in the society! I can't talk to you anymore. I thought we were best friends! Boy I was soooo wrong!" Billie turns and walks away.

"Billie! Billie! Don't be like that!" Billie can hear Tianna pleading behind but kept walking away, so nobody can see her watery eyes. Even Ti-ti is turning on me. Doesn't Abigail have enough worshippers, she has to take my one and only friend too? Skinny bitch is ruining my life as always. Life is just not fair for little people like me. Then she hears a familiar voice in the back.

"Hey Billie! We keep running into each other!" Billie turns back, it's Conner. Ugh she is not in the mood to entertain whatever Conner has in mind. "Hey what's up Conner. Aren't you supposed to go basketball practice?" Billie tried to avoid looking at Conner directly. Is he going to bring up the cafeteria incident? Or is he here to make fun of the audition? "Oh yeah, I am on

我，成為妳的閨蜜？」恬娜皺著眉頭，試圖解釋：「嗯，是的，其實艾碧愷會協助推廣這個課程。我們需要很多人的投入，一起來推動這個計畫。我們也需要妳啊，比莉。」恬娜顯然越描越黑，比莉怒不可抑：「我們？哇！艾碧愷和妳已經成了一個『我們』陣營了？她現在已經成為妳新世界裡的一份子啦？哈！聽起來，偉大的艾碧愷與恬娜二人組已經獲得眾人支持，準備大展身手一起完成一份小計畫呢！妳不需要我了。恭喜恭喜哦，改造社會，貢獻良多哦！抱歉，我沒辦法再跟妳說下去了。我還以為我們是好朋友，顯然是我看錯了！」比莉悻悻然轉身離去。

「比莉！比莉！不要這樣嘛！」比莉聽到恬娜在後方苦苦哀求，但仍疾步前行，她不願任何人看見她奪眶而出的淚水。現在竟連恬恬也背叛我了。拜託，艾碧愷的崇拜者還不夠多嗎？她非得把我唯一的閨蜜也奪走嗎？討厭的紙片惡女，一如以往毀了我的一切。我們這些微不足道的小人物也太可悲了，人生真是太不公平了。哀怨自憐的比莉，忽然聽到背後傳來熟悉的聲音。

「嘿，比莉！真巧啊，怎麼又遇到妳了！」比莉回頭看，是康納。心煩意亂的當下，面對康納的問候，比莉實在無暇理會，隨意虛應幾句：「嗨，康納！你怎麼會在這裡？不是該在球場練球嗎？」比莉岔開話題，不想直視

my way to the school gym. Hey, you wanna come watch us? Could use an extra pair of eyes to see if our defense is tight enough. You know, from an outsider's view." Billie is relieved that Conner didn't bring up either of the incidents. However in the corner of her eyes she can see Tianna from 20 feet away, staring at her and Conner chatting. Hmph, revenge time. You hangout with Abigail, then I will hangout with your beloved Conner. "Sure thing! I'll walk with you!" Billie smiles at Conner, holds his arms and walks towards the school gym. She can feel the burn from Tianna's stare...but she doesn't care, serves her right.

Later that evening at home after another frozen supper, she pulls up the phone. Aha! The app! She clicks on it immediately and is greeted by Starr. "Hi Billie! We meet again! Ready to post another one?" Oh no way, not until I figure this app out, you sneaky little AI robot! Billie is determined that there must be a way to delete her old posting. She found the "About" section and searched for Frequently Asked Questions. "... After the initial video has been produced, the old posting can be deleted by posting a new video." She screams with excitement. "YES! I figure out how to delete this stupid video!!!" She clicks back to Starr's "Post New Video" button. "Hi

康納，卻又忍不住臆測：「康納是不是想提起學校餐廳的那件事？還是想嘲笑我試奏會的醜態百出？」康納答：「哦，對呀，我正要去學校的體育館。嘿，妳想過來看我們練球嗎？或許妳可以幫忙觀察，看看我們的防守做得夠不夠。妳也知道啊，旁觀者清嘛。」看來康納並未提起比莉的心頭大事，比莉頓時感覺輕鬆多了。談話之際，她的眼角餘光清楚瞥見距離六米之外的恬娜，正眼睜睜盯著自己與康納攀談。太好了，大復仇的好時機。妳和艾碧愷走在一塊兒，那我就和妳心愛的康納玩在一起。「好啊！我和你一起去！」比莉對著康納嫣然一笑，挽著他的手臂，並肩向學校體育館走去。她似乎可以感受到恬娜又羨又嫉的眼光與心情……但比莉豁出去了，管她的，她活該！

當晚回到家，又是一頓冷凍食物加熱的晚餐。吃完飯，比莉拿起手機。啊哈！那個應用程式出現了！二話不說，趕緊點開，星兒隨即現身螢幕，向比莉熱情問候：「嗨，比莉！我們又見面了！準備好要再上傳另一則貼文了嗎？」啊，別想！在我還沒摸透這應用程式的底細之前，你這隻狡猾的小小人工智慧，別想再耍我！我可不會輕易上當了。比莉堅信，總能找到一個刪除舊文的方式。她找到一個「關於網頁」的欄目，再循序漸進，找到「常問問題」的下方，有段內文寫道：「原始錄影檔製成後，

Billie, looks like you are ready for a new post! Enjoy!" Starr shows the same old white box after a brief greeting. Hm, what should I post? Ah, let's do an expose posting about how lame the school band is.

He Who Denies All Confesses All

"May 30th, 2019. Catelyn's father used his influence as the city mayor, bribed Mrs. Hans and the school board to decide that only the privileged students in school could be in the school band. Lots of talented students auditioned, such as myself, but none of them were accepted. As it turned out, auditions were held for formality only, the band members were pre-determined behind closed doors. If the real talents cannot be in the band, joining the band is a pure joke. I'm glad that I'm not in this lame band."

OK, we make it short and sweet, to the point this time. Post. Starr shows up again, happy and enthusiastic as ever, "Thanks for the new post! We're working on it, will be done by midnight." Again he disappears and took the app icon with him. Billie feels pretty good this time, she kept her post tight and short, to the point and not lingering on conversations. And this will also explain to other people why she is not in the band. It's not that

可以透過上傳新影片的方式，來刪除舊影片。」她如獲至寶，興奮尖叫。「耶，太好了！我找到方法了！終於可以刪除那愚蠢的影片了！」她跳回星兒的網頁：按下「公布最新影片」的提示。「嗨，比莉，看來妳已準備好要放上新影片囉！好好享受！」星兒在一連串簡潔問候後，和上一次一樣，秀出了一個白色框框。嗯，我這一次要放什麼內容上去呢？啊……，有了，就放一個和學校樂團有關的內容吧，揭發樂團內部的醜陋真面目！

欲蓋彌彰的影片檔案

「2019年5月30日。柯特琳的爸爸以市長身份與勢力，賄賂漢斯教練與學校董事部，背地裡做出決策，規定只有學校裡的特殊分子才能獲准加入學校樂團。很多擁有音樂天分的學生雖然都報名參加試奏會，我也是其中一員，但我們這些資質甚優的學生，都沒有被選上。回頭檢視，所謂試奏會，不過是一場形同虛設的場子，做做樣子而已，真正的樂團成員早在黑箱運作的過程中，關起門來內定了。如果真正有才華的學生因為沒有後台關係而被阻擋於門外，那麼，加入樂團就是徹頭徹尾的一場荒謬劇。我很慶幸自己不是這種爛樂團的成員。」

這一次，我就讓這段紀錄精簡，點到為止。我按下

she's not talented, but the audition is rigged and she has no chance. Even better, it will get rid of her old video. She went to sleep with a big smile on her face.

Early morning. Billie wakes up super early, giddy with anticipation to watch her new masterpiece. "Hi Billie! Ready to watch your new post?" Starr presents her with the good news. Oh yes I am! The video starts.

Dark auditorium. "Next up, Billie Lin!" Billie walked up to the stage. She was trembling, fiddling with her saxophone. "Billie Lin, you need to announce your song choice. Points off." Billie closed her eyes and started playing the saxophone. However... unlike how Billie remembers, Billie in the video kept playing the wrong notes. And she was borderline squeaky from the very beginning.

When Abigail and Catelyn stood up and walked out, nobody else noticed their exit. Billie can hear her saxophone sounding weaker and weaker by this point.... Billie remembers this was when she was about to make that super loud squeak..... Oh no, here it comes. But in contrary to her memory, that one squeak wasn't really that bad. In the video, Billie looked stunned and stopped playing after the one squeak. She stood on the stage, staring blankly, for 5 minutes. The auditorium was dead

「發布」的確認鍵，檔案上傳成功。星兒再度出現，一如以往地活潑與熱情洋溢：「感謝妳的貼文。我們現在立即開始製作，天亮以前就會完成囉。」說完便消失，同時把程式標誌也一併帶走。比莉的感覺比上一次踏實多了，她把那篇文章寫得簡潔有力，痛下針砭又沒有太多冗長的對話。這麼一來，她也有個好理由來對外解釋自己何以不被樂團錄取；問題不在她的資格或音樂天分，癥結點是，這場試奏會根本在做表面功夫，害她不得其門而入。如果能藉此把舊的那篇影片刪除，那這個計畫真是完美得天衣無縫。那一晚，比莉心滿意足地入眠。

隔天清晨，比莉起了個大早，滑開螢幕，懸懸而望，拭目以待自己的傑作。「嗨，比莉！準備好要觀賞妳最新製作的影片了？」星兒跳出來，向她報告好消息。喔，當然！滿心期待呢！影片開始播放。

昏暗的禮堂。廣播傳來：「下一位演出者，林比莉！」比莉走上舞台。她緊張得渾身顫抖，開始撥弄著手上的薩克斯風。「林比莉，妳得先報告妳選的曲目哦，扣分。」比莉閉上雙眼，開始吹奏薩克斯風。但是……怎麼影片裡的情節，與比莉記憶中的畫面有所出入呢？在影片裡的比莉，吹奏過程不斷按錯音，整首歌幾乎不成曲調。其實打從一開始她彈奏出的每一個音，都在殘破的「嘎吱

quiet for a full minute and half before the audiences started whispering. "Billie Lin, you may leave the stage now." Mrs. Hans announced on the speaker. Billie walked like a zombie off the stage. End of video.

Billie is stunned and quite upset. That's not what I posted. I didn't post anything about my audition. How does this app know what happened? Also that's now how I remembered about the audition. I was playing well until Abigail and Catelyn ruined my performance! Wasn't I? Starr shows up again, "Hope you like the new video! We can only keep one post at a time, so your old video will be removed. Come back later for a new post!" and again disappears in Ethernet along with the app.

Billie sits fuming on her bed, regretting about the new post that will remind everybody of her miserable audition. Her situation just spiral from extremely bad to wickedly cursed, with no chance of recovery. She looks at the phone. 7:32AM. OMG I'm running late! Where's Tianna, why isn't she here yet? She looks out at the window, hoping to see Tianna waiting downstairs. Then a sharp pain shot her in the head with reality: She and Tianna are not talking anymore. Well, good riddance, I rather be by myself anyway.

Billie walks as fast as she can to school, but she is

嘎吱」與完整的音符之間，交替出現。

當艾碧愷和柯特琳起身走出去時，現場根本沒有人注意到她們的離去。此時，比莉聽到她的薩克斯風吹得越來越有氣無力……。比莉記得她是在她們兩人離去的剎那間發出那致命而響亮的「嘎吱」聲……哦，天啊，快到了，我不敢聽……不過，這一次的影片畫面，又與她原來的記憶迥然不同，那一聲「嘎吱」其實沒有想像中的慘不忍睹。在影片裡，比莉經過這一聲之後，錯愕又受挫地僵在原地，立即停止吹奏。她怔怔地站在台上，不知所措地發愣了五分鐘。前一分半的時間裡，全場鴉雀無聲，之後才開始出現交頭接耳、竊竊私語的狀況。「林比莉，妳現在可以下來了。」漢斯教練對著麥克風宣佈。心灰意冷的比莉，像行屍走肉的殭屍，步下舞台。影片結束。

比莉驚詫又懊惱。不！那不是我放上去的內容嘛，根本與事實不符。我隻字未提自己的試奏會啊。這個程式又從哪裡知道這些過程呢？而且，那些情節與畫面，也和我的記憶相去甚遠啊。我記得自己一開始吹得很好呢，本來就是被艾碧愷和柯特琳毀了我的表現，不是嗎？星兒又出現了。「希望妳對我們製作的影片感到滿意！我們每一次只能保留一則貼文，所以，之前的舊影片會被刪除。稍晚記得再回來分享新的貼文！」星兒說完，隨即與應用程式

still a few minutes late. On the way, Jake Khan walks up to her. "Hey, saw your post. Better luck for next year's audition, yeah?" Billie's face turns bright red. She wants to ask Jake more about the app, but he quickly walks away. Cameron is waiting for her at the front gate. "Hey Miss Squeaky. I need to talk to you. Meet me in room 203 right before lunch."

一同消失於螢幕上。

比莉的情緒不斷堆疊，火冒三丈的她一時之間也無計可施，困在那兒呆坐床上，懊悔自己不該把那篇新的貼文送上去，剛才那則新影片，只會提醒大家她在試奏會上醜態百出！簡直是雪上加霜！她盯著手機發呆，七點三十二分，哦！我的天啊！快遲到了！恬娜跑哪兒去了？她不是該跑來我家叫我嗎？比莉探頭往窗外望，心想會像往常那樣，看到恬娜在樓下等她。猛然記起了什麼，比莉心頭一震，一股回到真實世界的殘酷與失落，像尖銳的針，刺痛了她：是啊，她和恬娜已經形同陌路，兩人不說話了。好吧，總算擺脫她，算了算了，也好，我寧願獨自一人。

比莉快步往學校走去，到校時還是遲到了幾分鐘。途中遇到傑克，兩人擦身而過時，聽到對方丟下一句話：「嘿，看到妳的影片了。祝妳明年試奏會運氣好一點，加油哦！」比莉一聽，漲紅著臉，不知如何回應。她本想問傑克有關那個應用程式的其他細節，但傑克走得太快，一溜煙便不見蹤影，她追不上。到校時，倒見到卡麥龍在校門口等她。「嘿，嘎吱小姐。我需要跟妳談談。午休吃飯前，在203教室等我。」

第三章
CHAPTER 3

卡麥龍同學
Cameron

Room 203. Billie waits with anticipation. She is eager to tell Cameron about how she replaced the old posting with the new video, but worried that Cameron will make fun of her new video regardless. Cameron shows up a few minutes late. "Hey Cameron, can you stop calling me 'Miss Squeaky'? It was embarrassing enough, don't need you to remind me how bad my playing is." Billie wants to make sure she has the first word in. Cameron smiles and pulls up a chair. "You know, I almost forgot about that audition. Until you reminded me with your new post." Billie's face turns red hot. "You.... You watched the video already?" "Of course. I gotta keep track of your new posts so you'll keep your promise. But we're not here to talk about that." Oddly Billie is not too upset about Cameron seeing her new video. She rather Cameron sees it than anybody else in the world. She leans towards Cameron, her eyes wide open and signals Cameron to tell his story.

Cameron looks at Billie briefly, then shakes his head. "Obviously you are only paying attention to your own life, Miss Squeaky. I also posted a new video. Actually, it's a revision of my old video, which is quite interesting that you are allowed to do that. You know, sometimes you need to look outside of your own little world." Billie

203教室。比莉迫不及待要告訴卡麥龍她的新發現——以新貼文取代舊影片！可她也隱然擔心，卡麥龍會不會拿她的新影片來嘲笑她？卡麥龍比預定時間晚了幾分鐘才現身。「嘿，卡麥龍，你可以不要再叫我『嘎吱小姐』嗎？有夠尷尬的，好嗎？你不需要一直提醒我出糗的狀況有多糟糕，拜託！」見面一開始，比莉先表態，把話說清楚。卡麥龍臉上掛著笑容，拉了一張椅子，不疾不徐地說：「你知道嗎，我幾乎已經忘了那場試奏會，一直到你上傳了那個新影片，才又重新喚醒我的記憶，讓我想起當天的情境。」比莉面色鐵青：「你……你已經看了那個影片？」「當然！我怎麼可以錯過妳的任何最新貼文和影片呢？我要緊緊追蹤妳，才可以確保妳是否乖乖遵守承諾啊。不過，我們今天並不是要討論這話題。」奇怪，比莉發現自己竟開始有些寬心，也不太惱怒了，畢竟，如果可以選擇，她寧可看的人是卡麥龍，而不是其他任何人。她稍微傾身靠過去，瞪大雙眼，暗示卡麥龍可以開講了。

卡麥龍漫不經心地瞥了一眼比莉，搖頭輕嘆。「顯然妳只活在自己的世界裡，只關注自己的事啊，嘎吱小姐。嘿，妳知道嗎，我也上傳了一段新影片欸。其實，那是針對舊影片的修訂，這項功能還挺有意思的。妳知道的嘛，有時候妳需要從一個局外人的角度來檢視自己內在的小世

squints. "What do you mean, a revision of your old video? I thought you can only replace an old video with a new video." Cameron smirks and sits back. "Not exactly. I learned that there is an option to let you edit your old posting. Again, if you paid more attention to the rest the world other than yourself, you'll discover that option as well." Cameron lectures Billie, but for some reason Billie doesn't mind at all. The fact that you can edit old posts is just very exciting. She stands up clapping. "Oh my god, there is still hope for me!" She realizes Cameron's annoyed look. Oops that is about me again.

Billie gives Cameron a guilty look and sits down in front of him again. "Sorry I didn't watch your new video. So how did it come out? I was upset this morning with.... Um it's nothing. Just didn't have time to watch it." Billie vaguely remembers that Starr did mention something about Cameron's new video post when she was upset at Tianna not stopping by in the morning. Cameron crosses his arms. "How the video came out doesn't matter. But I think I figured out some parts of the AI behind the video posting. Yeah." Cameron smiles with a long gaze out of the window, nodding proudly.

Billie forcefully pulls his head back towards her. "Cameron! Don't just sit there and savor whatever you

界。」比莉蹙眉瞇眼，一臉困惑。「什麼意思啊？舊影片的修訂？我以為你只能用新影片來取代舊影片。」卡麥龍詭祕一笑，洋洋自得，下意識地將身體往後靠。「不一定哦。我發現其實可以選擇修訂與重新編輯自己的舊影片。我得再說一次，妳如果也稍微注意一下自己以外的世界，妳也會和我一樣，發現那個選項。」卡麥龍對比莉曉以大義，但比莉其實沒有把卡麥龍的「訓誨」放在心上。「重新編輯舊影片」的消息，讓比莉喜出望外。她情不自禁起身，拍手叫好：「哦！謝天謝地，我還有希望！」比莉的反應招來卡麥龍的白眼。哎呀，我又只想到自己了。

比莉有些不好意思地看著卡麥龍，一臉歉意地坐回椅子上，重新面對卡麥龍。「抱歉，我沒有看到你的新影片。所以，成果如何？我今天早上很不開心，因為……嗯，沒事啦。就是沒時間去瀏覽。」比莉依稀記得星兒似乎提及有關卡麥龍的新影片，但當時她正為著恬娜沒有到她家樓下而悶悶不樂。卡麥龍雙手抱胸，好整以暇地說：「影片呈現的效果如何，其實不那麼重要，但我想我已經找到解決方式，和影片背後的人工智慧相關的特質。」卡麥龍邊微笑邊往窗外凝視良久，胸有成竹地點點頭。

比莉用力將卡麥龍的頭轉向她，恨不得將他一把搖醒。「卡麥龍！別坐在那裡自我陶醉，你得趕緊和我分享

did, you have to share with me! We're in this together, remember?" Cameron glances back at Billie with a long sigh. "Again about you. All right. Why don't you stop by my house after school, I'll show you how to edit it." He stands up and walks out. Thank goodness. There is finally a way out of this mess. After that, I'll never have to talk to this egotistic jerk again. The nerves of him accusing me of being self centered! "Oh by the way," Cameron steps back as Billie is about to stick her tongue out behind his back, "If you get to my house before I do.... Watch out for my little brother. Last weekend he snuck out of the house to a party so he's grounded all week, and probably is in a grouchy mood." Billie quickly swallows her tongue and gives Cameron a fake smile and a thumbs up.

The Other Side of Cameron

After school. Billie follows the direction to Cameron's house, which is in a quaint neighborhood. He is probably the only one popular kid in school who is not from a rich family. Billie rings the doorbell. A little kid answers the door, checks out Billie from head to toe and gives her a dirty look. "Ugh. Another one of Cam's groupies? He's still practicing, you should know that.

啦！我們在同一條船上，記得嗎？」卡麥龍盯著比莉，無奈地長嘆一口氣：「唉，又只想到妳自己。好吧，那妳放學後可以到我家來一下，我可以示範給你看，教妳如何重新編輯與修訂。」卡麥龍說罷，起身離去。感謝老天爺！找到解決之道！我出運了！只要一切撥雲見日，我就可以甩掉所有狗屁倒灶的事，永遠再也不必和這個超級自私的白癡接觸了。真是無恥到極點，居然還批評本姑娘太自我！比莉正想要在他身後吐舌做鬼臉之際，卡麥龍忽然停下腳步，轉過身來，叮囑再三：「哦，對了，順便提醒妳，如果妳比我先到我家……小心我的小弟。上週末他偷偷跑出去參加舞會，所以這整個禮拜都被禁足在家。他現在的心情很鬱卒，臭脾氣可能一觸即發，妳自己小心點兒。」比莉收斂起鬼臉的舌頭，皮笑肉不笑，對著卡麥龍豎起拇指，表示了解。

卡麥龍的另一面

　　放學後。比莉往卡麥龍的家走去，那是個老舊的社區。看來，卡麥龍極有可能是學校赫赫有名的風雲人物中，唯一出身「非富裕家庭」的同學。比莉按電鈴。有個男生應聲開門，面對眼前這位客人，男生肆無忌憚地對比莉上下打量一番，再給她一個不屑的鬼臉。「哦，又一

Come back later." This must be his younger brother. Such a snobby little kid. "I'm not one of his groupies, thank you very much. He told me to come by, and I don't care if he's here or not I'm going to wait in his room. Otherwise I'll tell your teacher how you snuck out of the house to a party last weekend." The little boy looks at Billie with shock and a little tremble, full of disbelief. Is this random stranger a wizard in disguise? Or maybe she is the devil herself? How is it possible that she knows about his little rendezvous? He unwillingly lets her in the house and leads the way to Cameron's room while murmuring, "You are just bluffing. I bet you don't know anything."

Billie steps inside Cameron's room. His room is neat and tidy with a single color scheme – white. Everything is in perfect orderly state. All his notebooks are perfectly lined up on the desk, his bookshelf is organized from tall to short, the basketball posters are leveled on the wall, and the trophies on the shelves are in chronological order, evenly spaced out. Billie thinks of her own room there is always clothes on the floor, magazines and text books all over her bed, lots of random posters of rock stars, dogs and cats, newspaper clippings of her father's jazz band on the walls, and various sizes of wall paper

個卡氏粉絲嗎？妳應該知道他還在練球吧？晚點才會回來！」這小傢伙應該就是卡麥龍的弟弟，好個目中無人的的傲慢小屁孩。「感激不盡，但我不是他的粉絲哦。他要我過來一下，我不管他是不是在家，反正我在他房間等他就對了。不然的話，我就去告訴你的老師，你上禮拜偷溜出去參加派對的事。」小傢伙一臉詫異，難以置信地盯著比莉，不由自主地顫抖了一下，眼前這號人物怎麼對自己的事了若指掌啊？難道她是個偽裝的巫婆？或根本就是女妖魔啊？小傢伙嘴裡嘟噥著，心不甘情不願地開門讓比莉進到屋子裡，再把她引到卡麥龍的臥室。「別以為我不知道，妳只是在嚇唬我罷了。我保證妳什麼都不懂。」

比莉對小屁孩的回應置之不理，逕自走進卡麥龍的臥室。卡麥龍的臥室收拾得乾淨整齊，井然有序，房裡單一的白色系，讓整個空間看起來更簡潔明亮。他所有的筆記本堆疊在桌上，排序近乎完美，書架上的書，按著書型由高至低排列整齊，籃球海報並排貼在牆上，櫃子上的獎杯按著年份的先後順序擺放。兩相對照，比莉不禁想起自己的臥室——衣服總是亂丟地上，床上散置著雜誌與課本，牆上貼滿雜亂無章的海報，包括搖滾明星的照片、貓狗動物圖、與爸爸的爵士樂團相關的報紙報導；連天花板都被大小不一的壁紙樣本占滿。

samples on the ceiling.

Cameron walks in as she stares at photos of his basketball tournaments. "Hey Billie. Sorry the practice went a little longer today." Billie is a little taken back, hearing Cameron apologizing is a first. "Um no problem, it's okay, I'm a little early." She stutters. Cameron looks at the wall of photos from his various tournaments. "My dad wanted to make sure that I have a safety net, just in case my grade itself is not enough to get into a good college. He thought that basketball scholarship was a good way to augment my school work. I've been training and playing since 5. It's pretty pathetic that I don't have anything else going on with my life." Cameron laughs at himself.

"Anyway. Let's work on that app, shall we?" He pulls out his phone and clicks on the app. Billie sits next to him, staring closely at his phone. Cameron skips all the Starr greetings and chit chats, and goes right into the "post new video" button. "See here? There is an 'information' link, if you click on it, it takes you to an 'edit' page." He clicks on the link, and a white box shows up. Billie can see there are paragraphs inside the white box. Billie asks Cameron, "Hey, can I see your new video?" Cameron hesitates. "Cameron King, you

卡麥龍走進房裡時，比莉正盯著幾張卡麥龍參加籃球比賽的照片，看得出神。「嘿，比莉。對不起，讓你久等了，今天練球時間拖得比較晚。」比莉有些受寵若驚，還是頭一遭聽到不可一世的卡麥龍致歉呢。「哦，沒事沒事，是我早到了。」比莉有些不自在，結巴地回應。卡麥龍看著牆壁上好幾張不同的籃球賽照片，一邊說：「我爸爸要我把運動表現顧好，為了確保萬一我的學科成績不夠理想，進不到好大學，至少籃球成績可以扶我一把。我爸認為，籃球獎學金可以強化我的學校表現，成績單拿出來時會比較亮眼。我從五歲開始就接受籃球訓練了。我有時覺得自己蠻可悲的，這一生除了籃球還是籃球，其他沒什麼值得一提的。」卡麥龍自我解嘲。

「不說了。讓我們先來處理一下那個程式吧。」卡麥龍言歸正傳，取出手機，點開應用程式。比莉坐在他身旁，全神貫注地看著卡麥龍的手機。卡麥龍跳過所有星兒的問候與聊天片段，直接切到「上傳新影片」的按鈕。「看到這裡嗎？這裡有個『資訊』連結，妳如果點開，就會到『編輯』的頁面。」卡麥龍說罷，點開連結，出現一個白色框框。比莉看到格子裡寫了幾行文字。比莉轉頭問卡麥龍，「嘿，我可以觀賞一下你的新影片嗎？」卡麥龍猶豫了。「卡麥龍先生，你說你知道這個方法有效，那你

said you understand how this works now. So show me, it will make your explanation much easier to understand." Billie insists. Cameron rolls his eyes. "Fine. I do have to explain this after the video so you get the context. Don't want you to get the wrong idea." He clicks on "view video" button.

The video starts the exact same way. Cameron walked down the street and met the two bullies. The duo asked Cameron for money and Cameron promised by the weekend. Billie thinks, well, this is so far pretty much the same as before. What did he edit? But the video continues. After the bullies left, another boy walked up to Cameron. "I told you that you don't need to do this for me. It's my own business." Billie looks closer. It's Jake Khan, a freshman who is also in the basketball team. "Jake, we need you to focus on the practice. I'll take care of these thugs. They'll never leave you alone if I don't work it out with them." Cameron lectured Jake. Jake frowned. "I deal with this all the time, you don't think I can handle it myself? Mind your own business, Cameron. You're the co-captain for the basketball team, not my life." Jake stormed away. The video ends.

好歹得讓我見識一下嘛，這才有說服力啊，不然我要怎麼相信你呢！」比莉鍥而不捨。卡麥龍翻了個白眼。「好啦。我其實也需要在影片播放之後再跟妳解釋一些細節，妳才知道如何撰寫內容，我可不希望妳似懂非懂、一知半解。」卡麥龍點開了「觀賞影片」的按鈕。

內容的開場，幾乎和原來情節一模一樣——卡麥龍走在路上，碰見兩個欺負他的小流氓。混混雙人組跟卡麥龍討錢耍賴，卡麥龍承諾週末再給。比莉心想，嗯，這些片段和原來劇情幾乎沒差多少。那他到底修訂和編輯了哪些？影片持續播放，當小混混離開後，另一個男生出現，走向卡麥龍，說道：「我已經跟你說過了，你不需要為我做這些。這是我自己的事。」比莉目不轉睛地趨近螢幕，想看清楚那男生是何方人物。啊，那是傑克，是新生，也是籃球隊隊員。「傑克，我們需要你將心思放在練球上，全力以赴。這些惡棍和狗屁倒灶的事，我來處理就好。如果我不出面解決，他們是不會輕易放過你的。」卡麥龍對傑克說了一番道理，但傑克似乎不領情，不以為然地說：「這種事我經常都在處理，你覺得我自己沒能力解決嗎？你別多管閒事了，卡麥龍。你只是籃球校隊的副隊長，少在那裡指點我的人生。」傑克氣呼呼地走開。影片結束。

Blackmail & Secret

Billie looks at Cameron very confused. Cameron takes a deep breath. He opens his eyes halfway and glances sideway at Billie, patronizing her naiveness, as he deliberates:

"Squeaky, I will explain this. However our pact still stands, you cannot tell this to anybody." Billie holds out her pinkie towards Cameron with a dead serious face. "I pinky swear. Your secret is safe with me. Until the day I die." Cameron laughs, "Let's see if you can keep it till you're 90 years old! OK."

"One day at school, I was walking out of gym after practice. I heard a commotion in the hallway, and walked over to see what's going on. It was Jake Khan with the duo. I listened for a bit to see what's going on, and it turned out that the duo has found a note from Jake, addressed to Conner. It was an… admiration note, I guess. They threatened to show this note to everybody in the school. Jake looked helpless. You know, Jake is our freshman recruit, he's got tremendous potential in the team, I'm not going to let these thugs intimidate him like that. So I walked out, told them that I'll offer $100 bucks to buy that piece of note and they have to leave Jake alone. That's pretty much the back story."

一個被勒索的祕密

比莉百思不解，看得滿頭霧水。卡麥龍刻意吸了一口大氣，瞇著眼看著比莉，彷佛掌握天機，故意慢條斯理地說：「嘎吱小姐，我會解釋給妳聽。但妳要謹記我們之間說好的協定，守住祕密，無論如何，都不可以告訴任何人。」比莉舉起小手指，對卡麥龍作勢表達忠於承諾。「我向你發誓。我會守好你告訴我的任何祕密，絕不外洩，直到我死。」卡麥龍噗嗤笑出聲，「好吧，那就看看妳能不能守口如瓶到妳九十歲囉！」

「有一天在學校，我練完球後離開體育館。忽然聽到走廊附近傳來一些對話聲，好奇心驅使我走過去，想一探究竟。我看到傑克正和混混雙人組在講話，似乎在交涉些什麼。我想進一步了解到底是怎麼一回事，一聽之下，發現原來兩個小混混抓到了傑克的把柄，他們找到傑克寫給康納的字條，想要藉此來勒索他。嗯，以我的猜測，我想那是……一封情書吧。小流氓威脅傑克，要把那封情書昭告天下，讓全校都知道。傑克看起來非常無助。妳知道的嘛，傑克是我們球隊剛發掘的新手，也是我們球隊裡潛力無窮的球員，我說什麼都不可以讓這些流氓來威脅他。所以，我不得不出面，告訴這兩個混蛋，我會付一百塊來贖回那封信，而交換的條件是，他們不能再騷擾傑克。這些

Billie takes a deep sigh and sits back. "I had a feeling that Jake likes boys. It's not that big of a deal nowadays, you didn't have to pay off the bullies to keep that secret." Cameron frowns. "Are you kidding? We can't take any chance that our teammates getting distracted and being blackmailed by those bullies." "You can pay them off this time, but how many times can you do this? Jake is going to like boys forever, you know." Cameron goes into a deeper frown, then he shakes his head. "We're not here to talk about Jake. Let's get back to the app."

Billie reluctantly looks back at Cameron's phone. "Fine. What edits did you do to add that additional segment?" Cameron points to the paragraph in the white text box on the app. "The interesting thing is, in my original post, the video didn't match my writing at all. I didn't describe about the bullies or the blackmailing in my original post. I talked about the basketball practice and how we're going to the championship. You know, to inspire our team to practice. Then the video showed my meeting with the bullies, which was quite upsetting. Last night after I realized the opportunity to edit the original post, I wasn't sure how to edit. So I just added a second paragraph about what happened afterwards, the part when Jake came up to me after I talked to the bullies."

大概就是影片背後隱藏的故事。」

比莉倒抽一口氣，若有所悟。「我就覺得傑克喜歡男生。不過，現在男生喜歡男生已經沒什麼了，倒也不需要大驚小怪，你其實不需要花錢跟那兩個流氓交換這個祕密。」卡麥龍眉頭緊蹙，不以為然地辯解：「妳開什麼玩笑？我們絕不允許有任何萬一，一定會竭盡所能阻止那些流氓來恐嚇我們的隊員，不能讓他因為這件事而無法專心練球。」比莉回應：「這一次你可以用錢來解決，那下一次呢？當他們食髓知味了，你還可以讓他們得逞幾次？傑克還是會一直喜歡男生，這是事實啊，你應該很了解嘛。」卡麥龍眉頭鎖得更緊了，搖頭轉移話題：「我們現在不是要聊傑克。離題了，回到應用程式的問題吧。」

比莉只好放棄追問，回頭看卡麥龍的手機。「好吧。你是用什麼編輯修訂的步驟，去增加那段情節？」卡麥龍指著應用程式上白色框框內的段落。「有一點很令人費解，這些影片其實和我原來所寫的內容並不相符。我原先沒有寫到小混混跟勒索的部分，我寫的是有關籃球球隊的練習，還有我們為了籃球錦標賽怎麼辛苦和努力。妳了解的嘛，我想要激勵球員更用心練球。但是很奇怪，影片卻跑出我和小混混的交涉畫面，這真的很鬱卒、很無力欸。所以，昨晚當我發現了這個編輯修訂的方式，我其實也不

Billie smirks. "Really.... Is that really what you wrote? It's okay, you can tell me." But Cameron is dead serious. "Seriously. I decided to just write out exactly what happened. I mean, if the AI on the app can figure out what happened in real life, what is the point of lying about the truth?"

Billie is surprised. "Are you saying... you wrote how Jake reacted, and the video showed exactly that?" "Yes. That's the interesting finding on this app. If you write exactly what happened, it will create a video of exactly that."

Billie is very intrigued, but also skeptical about that statement. My statement about how the band audition is rigged is... somewhat true, otherwise how did Catelyn get in? But the app didn't transcribe how the auditions are rigged, and instead focused on my miserable audition. She purses her lips. "You know, I posted the truth about the school band audition process last night. But that's not what got posted. Let me show you."

Billie pulls out her phone and taps on the app and heads straight to "edit" link to show Cameron her post. "See, I simply described how the audition process is rigged, which is the truth. How can those privileged talentless girls like Catelyn get in the band? They bribed

太確定怎麼去修訂。我試著增加這段敘述，把背後隱藏的故事寫出來，就是妳剛剛看到的那些情節——當我和兩個小混混講完話之後，傑克跑來找我理論的那一段。」

比莉嘴角上揚，似笑非笑：「真的嗎……那真是你寫的內容啊？其實我很能理解的，你可以對我説實話，我可以接受哦。」卡麥龍義正言辭，嚴肅而認真。「真的啦。我後來決定實話實説，不再隱瞞。我的意思是，如果應用程式的人工智慧能發現與察覺真正發生的故事，那又何必大費周章去隱瞞真相呢？沒意義啊。」比莉很吃驚，恍然大悟。「你的意思是……你寫下傑克的反應，而影片就真的完全據實播出嗎？」「是啊！我發現這個程式最有趣的地方就在這裡。只要妳如實描述，它會製作一個完全符合實況的影片。」

這個發現引起比莉的好奇，但比莉仍對卡麥龍的説法有所保留，心存疑慮。我之前敘述過學校樂團只是表面功夫而已……就某方面來説，也是事實啊，否則柯特琳怎麼進得了樂團？不過，説也奇怪，這個程式怎麼絲毫沒有提及試奏會根本是一場虛張聲勢的假場子呢？不但完全跳過，還將重點都聚焦在我個人的試奏有多失敗，糗得很！比莉抿一抿雙唇，決定説實話：「你知道嗎，我昨晚將學校樂團試奏會的真實過程都上傳出去。但後來我看到的影

Mrs. Hans, it is pretty obvious."

Cameron looks at Billie with a cold expression. "Has it ever occurred to you that maybe...maybe Catelyn actually can play an instrument? And also, Miss Squeaky, you didn't just squeak one note. You were squeaky the whole entire song. I was there, I can attest to the video. You gotta look outside, pay attention to other people, stop being so self-centered."

Billie is offended by Cameron's statement, but she doesn't know how to respond. He's always accusing me of being in my own world! Does he not look at himself, always acting so self-righteous and know-it-all? He thinks Catelyn can actually play an instrument? Was my audition really that bad? What if Cameron is right? Can he actually be right about all of these?

片，卻和我寫的不一樣，簡直是天差地遠。我把影片找出來給你看。」

比莉拿出手機，點開程式，直接到「編輯修訂」的連結，再把影片播放給卡麥龍看。「你看，我就是直接撰寫試奏會的過程很形式化，我覺得那是事實啊。不然，像柯特琳那些毫無音樂天分的女生是怎麼被錄取的呢？她們賄賂漢斯教練嘛，再明顯不過了。」卡麥龍在一旁，冷眼看著比莉。「會不會有一個可能，是妳完全沒想到的狀況……也許，柯特琳真的會玩樂器？還有一點，嘎吱小姐，妳並非只發出一聲『嘎吱』哦。我當天也在現場，妳其實在演奏整首曲子的過程中不斷發出『嘎吱』聲，這方面我可以作證。妳其實需要從別人的角度看看這件事，稍微注意一下旁觀者或他人的觀點，不要老是把焦點放在自己身上，避免太自我中心。」

這下，比莉被卡麥龍激怒了，但又苦無策略去反擊。卡麥龍這傢伙怎麼老是批評我太封閉、說我活在自己的世界裡！什麼話嘛！他自己怎麼不反躬自問，反省一下自己啊，老是一副自以為是、無所不知的傲慢！他以為柯特琳真會玩樂器？還有，我的那場試奏會哪有如此不堪？但話又說回來，萬一卡麥龍的論點是對的呢？他對這些事件的理解與想法，有可能是對的嗎？

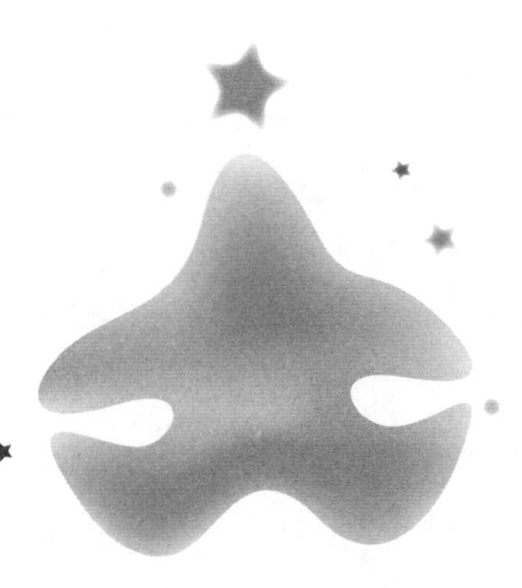

第四章
CHAPTER 4

砍掉重練
Do Over

Thursday after economics class. This is usually when school band practice takes place. Billie although despises the school band, but she is very curious about Cameron's accusation yesterday. There is no way that Catelyn can actually play an instrument! I need to see it with my own eyes. I'm going to record this, and go back to Cameron and tell him that he was sooooo wrong. He thinks he knows everything. I'm going to prove it to him that he doesn't! The thought of being able to tell Cameron that he was wrong in his face excites her as she marches down the hallway towards the band room. There is a little embarrassment to be openly trolling the band room as a band reject, so she carefully trolls the back hallway to make sure nobody sees her. Once the crowd dies out, she sneaks up to the back side of the room, cracks open the back door to take a peak inside.

"Quiet! From the top, please." She can see Mrs. Hans. The band starts playing the school fight song. Mrs. Hans points towards the wind section, and a flute solo follows. A nice crisp flute solo, hitting all the high notes with the perfect inflections and energy. Wow, that is a nice flute solo. The band has some talents! I wonder who that is? As much as Billie resents not being in the band, a good solo is a good solo. Years of listening to jazz

週四，經濟課之後通常是校內樂團練習時間。比莉雖然鄙視學校樂團，但一想起卡麥龍昨天對她的批評指教，倒令她心生好奇——柯特琳真的會玩樂器嗎？不可能！我得親眼見證。我還要錄下來給卡麥龍看，我要讓他知道自己錯得多離譜。哼！他還真以為是萬事通啊！我就是要把人證物證都備齊，讓他自慚形穢，讓他知道自己根本一無所知！一想到自己可以讓卡麥龍認錯到無地自容的歉疚神情，更激發比莉追根究底、揭發「真相」的決心。她步伐堅定，沿著長廊走向團練的教室。不過，身為樂團的反對派，這麼公然在團練教室外探頭探腦地四下張望，似乎有些不合宜。比莉心生一計，小心翼翼地繞到後方走廊，確保沒有其他人看到她。等進出的人群比較少了，她才躡手躡腳地躲到教室後方，偷開一點後門的門縫，窺探軍情。

「安靜！請大家從頭開始練。」比莉看得到漢斯教練。樂團開始演奏學校的加油曲目。漢斯教練指向管樂組，緊接著是長笛獨奏。這長笛吹得清脆悠揚，每一個高音都到位，抑揚轉折之間的力道，充滿穿透力。哇，長笛獨奏的功力，近乎完美呢，了不起！樂團裡畢竟還是有些資質不凡的成員啊！那位長笛樂手是誰呢？即便沒被樂團錄取對比莉而言是個打擊，但比莉長久以來在爵士樂團出身的爸爸身邊，耳濡目染下，也練就鑒賞音樂的品味與判

with her father has really taught her to appreciate good musicianship. "You see, Billie, flute is a hard instrument to master. It is an instrument that is commonly overlooked because of the simplicity of the sound, but to be able to capture audience with this simple instrument, a lot of technique and hard work is required to make it sound complex and haunting." Complex and haunting. That's a nice way to describe whoever is playing that magic flute.

Billie cracks open the door a little wider and leans in so she can see who is playing the solo. WHAT THE @#%$???? To her surprise -- It is Catelyn. She gasps, loses grip on the door knob, and reaches out to the door in attempt to keep her balance. The door makes a loud creak, swings open wide, Billie completely loses it and falls on the ground, making a loud "THUMP". The music stops, everybody in the band room turns back, and there is Billie -- on her arms and legs on the ground. Shit! Billie knows everybody's staring at her. She avoids eye contact with anybody in the room, stands up as fast as she can, and starts walking as if nothing happened. She can hear the roaring laughter in the band room as she exits into the hallway. Run away, Billie. As fast as possible. Worst day ever. Absolutely the worst. Now I

斷力，所以，比莉客觀評論，這長笛獨奏者真的很優秀。爸爸的一番話，言猶在耳：「比莉，妳看哦，長笛是個不容易駕馭、很難掌握的樂器。大家很容易忽略它，因為它的聲音聽起來單調，實在毫不起眼，所以，要如何以這麼簡單的樂器和音質來吸引觀眾的注意，需要花更長時間的練習來掌握好技巧，讓吹出來的聲音繁複渾厚，又餘音裊繞。」繁複渾厚而餘音裊繞。這形容詞，套用在那位吹奏神奇長笛的樂手身上，再貼切不過了。

比莉把門縫再撐開一點，緊靠縫隙邊，爭取多一些視角來看看那位長笛獨奏樂手是何方神聖。什麼？見鬼了！竟然是柯特琳？比莉震驚得無法言語，倒抽一口氣，下意識地鬆開緊抓門栓的手，她整個人靠在門上，奮力維持身體的平衡。但此時被撐開的門發出一聲巨響，瞬間隨風開啟，比莉的身體失去重心，頃刻間，一聲「碰」，比莉不偏不倚撲倒地上。教室內此起彼落的音樂聲，戛然而止，每一個人應聲回頭，數十雙眼睛盯著門後的不速之客——狼狽不堪的比莉，面撲倒地。天啊！還有什麼比這眾目睽睽的出糗更失態的嗎？太丟人現眼了！比莉二話不說，以最快的速度彈跳起來，避開眾人目光，轉身快速離開現場，然後，再假裝若無其事地放慢腳步往前走。她走到長廊外了，還聽到樂團教室傳來震耳欲聾的笑聲。比莉，跑

definitely don't want to be in the band, ever.

Then somebody calls her name in the hallway. "Billie! Billie Lin!" She looks back, it is Mrs. Hans. Ugh Mrs. Hans is going to yell at me. Don't make a scene, apologize and walk away. Billie stops and slowly walks back to Mrs. Hans. "I'm sorry Mrs. Hans, I...I won't do this again." Billie holds back her tears and fears, squeezes her eyes shut, and stutters her apology to Mrs. Hans. She's going to yell at me.... Here it comes.... Surprisingly, instead of a harsh scolding, Billie feels a gentle touch on her shoulder. It is Mrs. Hans' hand. "Billie. We're all disappointed that you are not part of the band. You didn't practice enough for the audition, it was very obvious. However... we really could use a good saxophone player. I'm willing to give you a second chance to audition for the band. But you better be really ready this time."

What. Just. Happened? Did she offer me a second audition? But with all those humiliation, I don't want to be in the band.... Billie responds with her head lowered and her eyes shut tight. "Nah Mrs. Hans, I'm good. I don't care about being in the band." Billie turns and walks away as fast as she can.

吧。竭盡所能地逃離這裡。這是最慘不忍睹的一天，史無前例的慘烈。從今以後，我永遠再也不想加入樂團了。

忽然，她聽到後方長廊有人呼叫她。「比莉！林比莉！」她轉頭看，是漢斯教練。哦，漢斯教練鐵定要來破口大罵了。可別讓老師有機會當眾飆罵，好漢不吃眼前虧，趕緊道歉再走開。比莉駐足轉身，緩緩走向漢斯教練。「對不起，漢斯教練，我不會再這麼做了。」比莉用盡全身力氣壓抑她的淚水與恐懼，緊閉雙眼，結結巴巴地吐出幾句道歉。完蛋了，她快要發飆了……快了快了……。怎麼回事？比莉等到的居然不是預期中的咆哮怒罵，而是肩膀上溫暖的撫慰。那是漢斯教練的手。「比莉，我們很遺憾妳沒有成為我們樂團的一份子。那天的試奏會很明顯，大家都看得出妳練習不足。但是……我們真的很需要一位優秀的薩克斯風團員。我想給妳第二次試奏的機會。不過，這一次妳得認真練習和準備。」

什麼？不會吧？剛剛發生什麼事了？老師再給我第二次試奏機會？可是，當眾出糗所引發的這一連串恥辱，我說什麼也不想加入樂團……。面對老師格外開恩的善意，比莉反而不知所措了，她低眉垂眼，輕聲回答：「嗯，漢斯教練，我很好。沒關係，有沒有被錄取加入樂團，我其實不在乎。」比莉轉身用最快的速度離開。

A Second Chance

Billie walks home alone, thinking about what Mrs. Hans said, "Second chance. You better be really ready. Good saxophone player." Her dad would be so proud of her if she joined the band. But she failed so miserably at the first audition, what if she's just not talented? Oh, who cares, she already told Mrs. Hans she's not interested. Then she notices a couple girls walking by, chatting with excitement. She looks over, it's Tianna with Abigail.

"Oh hi Billie." Tianna greets Billie, awkwardly. Abigail just smiles and says nothing. So there she is, hanging out with Abigail. Billie can't decide if she should stay and look cool, so she can show that she is not afraid of confronting Tianna and her newfound friendship with Abigail; or she should leave because she wants nothing to do with Tianna anymore. She stands there silently staring at her feet, trying to figure out what to say or do. The more she contemplates her move, the tighter her jaws clinch together and her legs freeze to the ground. She stands there silently staring at her feet, trying to unwind herself from this mess that she dragged herself into. But alas, in vain.

Tianna speaks again, "Hey Billie...We can still use your help on the poster." Billie is lost on words or action.

第二次機會

比莉獨自走回家，邊走邊思索漢斯教練所說的話——「第二次機會。這一次得要認真練習和準備。優秀的薩克斯風團員。」比莉心想，如果能加入樂團，爸爸一定非常以她為榮。但回想上一次的試奏會，她的表現簡直爛透了，醜態百出，難道，她真的毫無音樂天分？哦！不想了，管他呢，反正已經拒絕漢斯教練了，本姑娘沒興趣，謝謝再聯絡。比莉一抬頭，剛好瞥見兩個女生經過她身邊，兩人相談甚歡。她定睛一看，是恬娜與艾碧愷。

「哦，嗨！比莉。」恬娜尷尬地向比莉打招呼。艾碧愷在一旁微笑，沒說什麼。哦，原來她和艾碧愷玩在一塊兒了。比莉當下拿不定主意，到底要面不改色地從容應對，好證明自己一點也不在乎恬娜與艾碧愷發展的新友情；或者她該冷眼漠然，轉身就走，以示她與恬娜早已毫無瓜葛。但比莉的雙腳好似被釘牢了般，只能駐足垂首，沉默以對，心中卻百般猶豫，到底該說幾句話表態，或繼續默不作聲，但比莉始終拿不定主意。

恬娜再度開啟話題：「嘿，比莉……我們還是想要請妳協助設計海報。」比莉不曉得該如何反應，徹底無措。我到底該說什麼？拒絕幫忙？或說，妳和艾碧愷就可以解決啦，何必找我？空氣中瀰漫一股尷尬而死寂般的沉默，

What should I say? I don't want to help? Or you and Abigail can solve it? A very awkward minute passes where Tianna just stood there, waiting for Billie to say something. Abigail breaks the silence. "C'mon, let's go Tianna, we have a lot of work to do on your project." And grabs Tianna's arms and walks away. Tianna looks back at Billie as she walks away, Billie is still just looking at her feet.

Back home. "Billie my pumpkin!" Billie is surprised to see her mother at home, and not drunk today. She is in her fanciest outfit. "Hey kiddo. You know the drills – food in the fridge. I got a date tonight, won't be home till later. This one sounds like a rich guy, hopefully we can all move out of this dump to somewhere nicer! Wish me luck!" Her mother puts on lipstick and checks herself in the mirror before leaving the house. Ugh when she's not drunk she goes dating losers. Again nobody cares about me. Right then, her mother turns back to Billie as she heads out. "Oh almost forgot, your father wants you to call him." Dad? It's been ages since we talked last. What does he want now?

Billie pulls out the phone. Two missed calls, it says. Both from her father. She listens to the voicemail. "Hey Billie Millie! It's your dad. Haven't talked to you for a

持續了數秒，恬娜站在那兒等待比莉的回覆。一旁的艾碧愷為要化解僵局，挽著恬娜的手催促道：「走吧，恬娜，我們還有很多工作要完成呢。」恬娜邊走邊回頭看著比莉，比莉依然站在原處，低著頭，盯著自己的腳。

終於回到家了。「比莉啊，我可愛的小南瓜！」出乎預料，媽媽竟然在家，而且不但沒有醉酒，還很清醒地精心打扮，看來準備外出。「嘿，小寶貝，老規矩，記得吧？東西都在冰箱裡。我今晚有約，回來大概很晚了。今晚約會這傢伙看來像個富豪，真希望我們可以盡快離開這鬼地方，搬去更好的區域！祝我好運吧！」出門前，媽媽不忘再三攬鏡自照，塗上口紅，才悠然出門。唉，要嘛醉得不省人事，要嘛和魯蛇約會。反正，沒人會在乎我！已經踏出家門的媽媽，忽然想起了什麼，回頭轉向比莉說：「哦，我差點忘了，妳爸爸要妳打電話給他。」爸？我們好久好久沒有講過話了。他這一次又想怎麼樣了？

比莉把電話拿出來，一看，兩通未接來電。都是爸爸打來的電話。她打開語音留言。「嘿，比莉米粒！我是妳爸啦。好久沒跟妳講講話了，對不起啦，這陣子真的忙死了。我們的巡迴演出已經來到最後一檔了，再過幾個禮拜就會回到家，我想我們或許可以安排一下見面的時間？我在紐奧良的時候發現一個超級棒的薩克斯風吹嘴，是由爵

while, sorry I've been crazy busy. We're on the last leg of our tour now, will be back home in a couple of weeks, thought maybe we could spend some time together? I found this super awesome saxophone mouthpiece when I was in New Orleans, hand made by the Jazz legend himself. You'd love it! Call me when you get a chance!" Her dad plays the alto sax in the local jazz band, and they tour around the world performing in various venues since him and Billie's mom divorced. Billie has always wanted to be like her dad – talented and free spirited, not being stranded and tied down to this dump little apartment, not being harassed and belittled by skinny bitches at school. Billie calls her dad back. "The mobile user is not available at this time, please call back or leave a message." Billie hangs up.

Right then, "Ding!" The app shows up. "Hi Billie! Welcome back! Ready to post some more?" Starr shows up, as peppy as usual. Billie clicks on the "edit" button, and stares at her post from two nights ago. She thought about the scenes from the band room today. Catelyn was good. Maybe she bribed her way into the band, but maybe she didn't have to because she was really good with the flute. Mrs. Hans only likes skinny bitches in the band. But she also offered me a second chance audition,

士大師親手作的哦！妳一定會愛死了。妳方便的時候給我打通電話！」比莉的爸爸在當地一個爵士樂團擔任低音薩克斯風樂手，自從爸媽離婚之後，爸爸便跟著樂團，到世界各地的不同場合中巡迴演出。比莉一心想要像爸爸那樣——充滿音樂細胞，率性灑脱，無拘無束，不必受困在這個垃圾堆的小公寓裡，綁手綁腳的，更不必被學校的惡女霸凌羞辱。比莉回電給爸爸。「您所撥的電話沒有回應，請稍後再撥或留言。」比莉把電話掛了。

就在此時，「叮」，應用程式出現在螢幕上。「嗨，比莉！歡迎回來！準備更新上傳其他資料嗎？」星兒又出現了，永遠精力充沛的聲調和神情。比莉點開「編輯」按鍵，專注看著她這兩晚放上的貼文。今天發生在團練教室的情景，倏忽躍入腦中，比莉陷入沉思。嗯，柯特琳吹得真好。也許她靠賄賂才能加入樂團，也或許她大可不必，因為她吹長笛的功力實在很棒。我一直覺得，漢斯教練偏愛樂團裡那兩個紙片惡女。話雖如此，但漢斯教練卻願意再給我第二次試奏機會，所以，或許她並非我所想的那樣，偏心獨厚那兩個女的。這段被我徹底搞砸的人生，實在讓我不知所措，我已經不曉得人生該怎麼走下去了。不知為何，比莉忽然想起卡麥龍説的一段話，「如果妳把發生的事件據實以告，影帶就會如實呈現。」好，我想我可

so maybe she doesn't only like skinny bitches. I don't know what's going on in my screwed up life anymore. Then she remembers what Cameron said. "If you write exactly what happened, it will create a video of exactly that." I guess I can try that. She starts typing away."

I went to see who's all in the school band. Catelyn was there. They played the school fight song. I fell, they laughed, but Mrs. Hans offered me a second chance audition. I didn't want to be in the school band so I said no."

The Unbearable Honesty of Billie

Billie struggles, especially about the part when she fell. She attempts to re-write in various different angles so it's not as embarrassing, but Cameron's voice keeps ringing in her head: "write exactly what happened". Ugh Fine. My life can't get any lower than this, just do it. With great pain, she finishes the paragraph about her embarrassment and her refusal to Mrs. Hans's offer about the second audition.

She reads her new addition one more time, takes a deep breath, squints and clicks "submit post". Here goes more embarrassment, story of my life. I don't know why I'm listening to Cameron, so stupid. It is the most

以試試看。比莉開始埋頭書寫，敘述整件故事的重點。

「我去看看學校樂團的成員到底有誰。柯特琳在那裡。他們演奏學校的加油曲目。我撲倒在地，大家都哄堂大笑，但漢斯教練卻願意給我第二次試奏的機會。但因為我不想成為樂團一員，所以，我拒絕了。」

不堪又痛苦的誠實

比莉陷入天人交戰，尤其那段跌倒的敘述，她猶豫是否說出真相，試著從不同角度切入再重寫，試圖讓這段眾目睽睽下的超級醜態，多幾分修飾，少一點尷尬，但卡麥龍的提醒不斷縈繞耳中：「據實以告。」彷彿吞下百般屈辱再豁出去，比莉忍痛把當天發生的兩大重要事件如實記錄——她跌倒的糗事、拒絕漢斯教練二度試奏會的提議。

大功告成了，比莉再重讀自己寫的內容，深呼吸，然後，滑到網頁下方，按下「送出上傳」的連結。唉，拭目以待吧！最慘不忍睹的尷尬不過如此了！這就是我的人生故事。我不知道為什麼我要接受卡麥龍的意見？我太笨了。這真是比莉此生最痛苦不堪的社群媒體貼文——把自己最不堪入目的悲慘經歷昭告天下。比莉難過得忍不住痛苦呻吟，她把頭埋進手掌中，無以為繼。爬上床時，她暗自哀嘆，等著看我世界末日的影片吧。我的社交生活終將

painful social media post that she's ever done in her life: posting her own miserable experience. Billie groans and sinks her head deep inside her hands. Prepare for the doomsday video. My social life is over. As she craws into bed to sleep.

Early next morning. Billie reluctantly opens her eyes and reaches for the phone. Starr is already waiting for her on the app. "Hi Billie! Your video is ready!" Ughhhh. Do I really have to watch this. The video plays. She watches herself losing balance and falling on all fours in the band room. Mrs. Hans offered her a second chance. However, right after Mrs. Hans' offer for the second audition, the video zooms into Billie's face and plays in slow motion. She had a very, very faint excitement in her eyes, so subtle that only slow motion could capture the fleeting moment. The video ends before Billie's response to Mrs. Hans.

What happened to the ending where I declined Mrs. Hans? What's up with the slow motion of my face? Billie is too engrossed thinking about how the video ends, to think about the potential embarrassment this posting could bring. Especially about the last scene when she looked genuinely excited, for a sliver of a second. I wonder if Cameron's seen this. He might know what's

毀於一旦，從此再也抬不起頭了。

隔天一早，比莉勉強睜開雙眼，拿起手機，星兒早已在應用程式上等待。「嗨，比莉！妳的影片已完成囉！」啊！非看不可嗎？影片播放了。她看見自己在團練教室後方因身體失衡跌了個四腳朝天。漢斯教練提議比莉接受第二次試奏機會。然而，就在漢斯教練提出邀約當下，影片畫面放大聚焦於比莉臉上，再進入慢動作播放。畫面中的比莉，眼神閃過一絲激動，隱隱然的興奮之情，微弱得必須得靠慢動作特寫鏡頭，才能捕捉倏忽而過的剎那反應。播放到此結束，比莉拒絕漢斯教練的那一段，並未出現。

咦，我拒絕漢斯教練的畫面，怎麼沒出現？我臉部表情的特寫與慢鏡頭，又是什麼意思？比莉全神貫注思索新影片停格與結束的那一幕，一邊也擔心這個影片出現後，會造成什麼樣的風暴與難堪。尤其是最後一幕特寫鏡頭，畫面出現比莉臉上那一閃而過，掩不住的真摯與興奮之情。我很好奇卡麥龍是否看過這個影片，或許他可以替我解惑。我需要知道這到底是怎麼一回事。劍及履及，比莉立即換上衣服，跑到學校，希望可以在路上攔截卡麥龍。

午休時間。203教室。「所以，你覺得這是什麼意思呢？」在空無一人的教室內，比莉把最新的影片，以自己的手機播放給卡麥龍看。來到比莉臉部的特寫鏡頭時，比

happening. I need to understand what is going on. Billie gets dressed and runs for school, hoping to catch Cameron on the way.

Room 203 at lunch. "So what do you think this means?" Billie shows Cameron her new video on her phone in an empty classroom. She pauses the screen on her zoomed in face. "Why did the app decide to zoom in on my face? What is it trying to show? Why did it not play the last part of the post, where I said no to the second audition?" Cameron shrugs. "It could mean a lot of things, Miss Squeaky. Our pact is to keep each other's secrets, not to do forensic analysis on the AI." Billie contests. "Again I can't say this enough times, we are in this together. If we solve the algorithm behind the AI, we might be able to get out of this pact and your secret will be safe regardless of my action! Now focus and tell me what you think." She puts her phone in Cameron's face.

Cameron plays back the video a few more times. "Well, one thing is pretty clear. You seem to be excited in the video. And the AI decided not to include your response." Cameron strolls around the room, thinking. "One idea. Maybe you should do the second chance audition." Billie panics. "NO, absolutely not! I already said no to Mrs. Hans. I can't go back. Besides, I don't

莉按了暫停鍵。「我不明白，為什麼這個程式會把我的臉部表情特寫放大？它想要傳達什麼樣的意思嗎？我把漢斯教練提議的第二次試奏會邀請，以及我的拒絕，都寫在裡面了，但為什麼影片完全略過這段結論，沒有出現在螢幕上？」卡麥龍聳聳肩，不予置評，但不忘提醒比莉：「意思可以很多，嘎吱小姐。但我們之間的協議是彼此保密，而不是要替這個程式進行抽絲剝繭的分析。」比莉辯解道：「我還是要不厭其煩地提醒你，我們在同一條船上。只要我們能成功破解這個人工智慧背後的演算法則，我們或許就可以結束這場協議，不管我怎麼樣，你都可以守住你的名聲與形象，所有這些事件，都可以安全落幕。所以，現在，你要完全專注在這件事，然後告訴我你的想法。」比莉把手機放到卡麥龍眼前。卡麥龍有點被說服了。他把那段影片反反覆覆播放了好幾回，留心檢視每一個畫面。「嗯，有一件事是顯而易見的。畫面裡的妳似乎非常興奮開心。我想，人工智慧在製作時，決定不把妳的回應放進去。」卡麥龍在教室裡來回踱步，一邊思索推敲各種可能性。「我有個建議。或許妳應該接受第二次試奏會的提議。」比莉一想起就驚慌失措，立即反彈：「不！絕不！我已經拒絕漢斯教練了。我不能走回頭路。再說啊，我根本沒什麼天分。」卡麥龍以一貫盛氣凌人之姿，

have talent." Cameron rebukes with his usual snobby attitude. "Miss Squeaky, it is obvious that Mrs. Hans thought you are a good saxophone player. And it is obvious that you were happy to hear that you could have a second chance. The only thing that you don't have is enough practice."

The Courage To Challenge

Billie frowns, looks at her feet and murmurs, "I don't care about being in the school band. School bands are for losers." "Look, Billie, you have talent but don't like to practice. I have a few of those in my basketball team too. You know what I do with them? I stay with them and make sure they practice, so their talent can finally shine." Cameron starts walking out. "Speaking of which, I need to go practice. Good luck with the second audition."

Billie walks out of room 203, wandering around school hallways. "Ding!" It is a text from her dad. "Billie Millie, sorry I missed your call last night. Looking forward to seeing you when I'm back!" She immediately calls her dad. "Hi Dad?" "Oh hi my little jazz wonder! So great to hear your voice! Aren't you in class now?" "We're in recess now." "How are you doing? Sorry I

訓斥比莉：「嘎吱小姐，漢斯教練真的覺得妳是個優秀的薩克斯風樂手嘛！而妳一聽到還有第二次試奏的機會，妳也顯然很興奮啊，不是嗎？唯一的問題是妳練習不足。」

接受挑戰的勇氣

聽完卡麥龍這番解釋，比莉眉頭深鎖，低頭喃喃自語：「我不在乎能不能加入學校樂團。樂團裡都是一堆魯蛇，我不屑。」卡麥龍不以為然，他說：「比莉，妳聽我說，妳其實有天分，只是不喜歡練習。我的籃球隊裡也有一些像妳這樣的球員。妳知道我怎麼處理這個問題嗎？我留下來陪他們，確保他們好好練球，好讓他們的天分與球技最後都能充分發揮，發揮到淋漓盡致！」卡麥龍邊說邊往外走。「哦，說到這兒，我需要去練球了。我只能祝妳第二次試奏會演出成功囉，祝妳好運啊！」

比莉走出203教室，在走廊上若有所思地來回踱步。「叮」！手機傳來爸爸的簡訊。「親愛的比莉米粒，抱歉我昨晚錯過妳的來電。我非常期待回來後與妳見面的時刻！」她立即打電話給爸爸。「嗨，是爸嗎？」「哦嗨，我的爵士小神童！聽到妳的聲音真是太開心了！妳現在不是應該在上課嗎？」「現在是休息時間。」「最近過得怎麼樣啊？很抱歉我好久沒有和妳說說話了。學校生活一切

haven't talked to you so long. How is school? You're still playing saxophone, I hope? Got you this super awesome mouthpiece, it's going to blow your mind!" "Um. Yeah I still play. I-I'm trying out for the school marching band." Billie doesn't know why she lies to her dad about the band tryout.

"OMG you need this mouthpiece! When is the tryout? I'm going to see if I can get home sooner so you can have this mouthpiece for your tryout!" "Thanks dad. I-I gotta go. Love ya." Billie hangs up, but what Cameron said rings in her head. Cameron thought I should do the second chance audition. Should I? Dad will be so proud of me if I'm in the band. But... I did say no to Mrs. Hans. She aimlessly strolls down the school campus thinking about this over and over. I wish there is a sign that tells me what I should do. Then, in the middle of the school running track, she sees Mrs. Hans walking towards her. Billie's eyes light up. Whoa! This is a sign. That's it. Billie takes a deep breath, clinches her fist tight, and walks towards Mrs. Hans. All right, here goes nothing.

"Hi ! Mrs. Hans. I would like to take up on your offer and do a second chance audition."

都好嗎？我希望妳還繼續在玩薩克斯風，有吧？我一定要送妳這個超級棒的吹嘴，妳肯定會愛死它！」「嗯，是啊，我還有在吹薩克斯風。我還在努力，試試看能不能加入學校的樂團。」比莉搞不清楚自己為何要對爸爸撒謊。

電話那頭的爸爸興奮不已：「哦我的天啊！那妳肯定需要這個吹嘴！什麼時候試奏會？我安排看看或許能提早回家，那我就來得及把吹嘴給妳，讓它在試奏會時派上用場了。」「爸，謝謝你。我得走了，掛電話囉，愛你哦。」比莉結束與爸爸的通話，但卡麥龍說的那番話在她腦中盤旋，揮之不去。卡麥龍覺得我應該要給自己機會，接受第二次試奏會的提議。我該接受嗎？我若被樂團錄取，爸爸一定會為我感到驕傲。但問題是……我已經拒絕漢斯教練了。比莉漫無目的地往校園方向走去，反覆不斷想著剛剛與爸爸之間的對話。我真希望能忽然出現個神明顯靈或徵兆，給我指點迷津，告訴我該怎麼做。才這麼想著，一抬頭，竟看見漢斯教練從學校跑道正中央，朝著她走來。比莉瞪大眼睛，太不可置信了。哇！這就是最好的徵兆了！比莉深吸一口氣，緊握拳頭，勇敢大踏步迎向漢斯教練。好吧，沒什麼大不了的，冷靜。

「漢斯教練，我想接受妳提議的第二次試奏會。」

第五章
CHAPTER 5

練習練習再練習
Practice Practice Practice

Billie runs over to the school gymnasium, full of excitement and anxiety. OMG, what have I done? I just signed up for the second audition. It's all Cameron's doing. He OWES me! The basketball team is in full practice for the upcoming championship. Conner Sutherland dribbles the ball, makes a swift one and a half turn under the basket and jumps for the hoop. Cameron jumps up against Conner and stretches his arm high to block his aim. Conner immediately tosses the ball to nearby Jake, who quickly dunks in the hoop behind Cameron. Their coach blows the whistle. "All right everybody, good practice. Conner and Jake, good pass. Cameron, that was a weak jump, you gotta aim higher! Everybody pack up!" Conner notices Billie in the gym.

"Hey Billie! Good to see you! How do you think we're doing?" He walks over to Billie, sweaty and smiling. "Oh hi Conner, you guys look great! Definitely ready for the championship next week!" Billie fakes a smile and enthusiasm. Conner, not noticing her fake expression, smiles even wider. "Hey, you wanna walk home together? I have something to ask you. Let me go pack up, I'll be right back." Conner leaves before Billie can say anything. Billie looks around for Cameron. He is in the court picking up balls.

夾雜著爆表的興奮與忐忑，比莉載欣載奔地衝到學校體育館。我的天啊！我剛剛做了什麼創舉啊？我竟答應要參加第二次試奏會。哦，卡麥龍幹的好事！他應該感謝我呢！體育館內，籃球校隊正奮力加強練習，為即將到來的錦標賽摩拳擦掌。康納在運球，忽然以迅雷不及掩耳之勢轉身，蹲低再縱身一跳，對準籃筐，準備投球。卡麥龍騰空跳躍，伸展手臂企圖擋下康納的舉手投球。防禦來勢洶洶，對投球不利，康納機警地把球傳給身旁的傑克，傑克早已迅速從卡麥龍身後趁虛而入，接球，投籃。「嗶……」教練吹哨，說道：「好啦！大家今天都表現得不錯。康納和傑克，球傳得好。卡麥龍，你跳得不夠好，你的目標要設得更高才對！好啦，大家收一收，今天就到這裡！」康納注意到走進體育館的比莉。

「嘿，比莉！難得看到妳在這，很開心欸！妳覺得我們剛剛表現得怎樣啊？」汗流浹背的康納，笑逐顏開，緩緩走向比莉。「嗨，康納，你們很厲害！大家都進入最佳狀態哦，看來已經準備好要迎戰下週的籃球賽了！」比莉心不在焉，強顏歡笑，裝出一副興奮的樣子。康納並未留意比莉不太自然的表情，他把比莉虛應的話當真，而喜不自勝。「嘿，一起走回家好嗎？我有些事想問妳。妳等我，我去收一下東西，馬上就可以走了。」比莉還來不及

"Hey Cameron!" Billie walks over. "Oh, it's you. Hey." Cameron barely looks at Billie and continues to pick up balls scattered around the court. Billie cannot hide her excitement. "I'm doing it! I'm doing it! It's your idea, but I'm doing the second audition. I'm soooo nervous. What should I do? My second audition is on the 15th!" Billie follows Cameron as he continues to walk towards scattered balls in the corners. Cameron seems agitated, and yells at Billie. "What should you do? Practice, that's what you should do, and that's what I should do. Now go away, I need to practice." Billie is upset with his cold attitude about such an extraordinary accomplishment on Billie's part. "What do you mean you need to practice.... Aren't you guys done for the day? I, on the other hand, need lots of practice. Oh gosh I have only two weeks to practice before the audition! Do you think I should do the same song as last time, or should I try a new song?" Cameron stops, turns around to Billie and scolds: "Here you go again, just talking only about you. Have you ever thought of other people? I NEED TO PRACTICE!" and walks away. What's up with him? The nerves!

Conner walks Billie home. After a long pause between casual chats about school, movies, and

回應，康納已自顧自地跑開了。難得空檔，比莉環顧四周，尋找卡麥龍的身影。看到他了，卡麥龍在球場撿球。

「嘿，卡麥龍！」比莉走過去。「哦，是妳啊。」卡麥龍漫不經心地回應比莉，頭也不回，繼續把散置各處的籃球一一撿起來。比莉難掩興奮，迫不及待要把好消息告訴卡麥龍。「我答應了！我答應了！雖然是你的想法，但我已經答應老師要第二次試奏了。我真的超級緊張的！快炸開了！我接下來該怎麼辦呢？我的第二次試奏會是在十五號。」比莉緊隨卡麥龍身後，跟著他到處去撿球，一邊如連珠炮般說個不停。卡麥龍有些不耐煩，對著比莉怒吼：「妳該怎麼辦？練習啊，那就是妳該做的呀，那也是我該做的啊！妳現在走開啦，我要練球。」對比莉而言，這是多麼意義非凡的成就和決定啊，竟被卡麥龍澆了一盆冷水，比莉懊惱極了。「你還要練球？什麼意思啊？你們不是已經練一整天了嗎？我才真的需要練習欸。哦，媽呀，離試奏會只剩兩個禮拜，我得快馬加鞭了。嘿，你覺得我應該吹奏原來那首曲目嗎？還是，我該換一首新的曲子？」卡麥龍停下腳步，神色不耐地轉身教訓比莉：「妳又來了，眼中只有自己。妳有沒有替別人設想過啊？我告訴妳幾次了？我要去練球！」說罷悻悻然走開。這傢伙是怎麼了？發什麼神經啊，陰晴不定！

basketball, Billie asks, "So....what is the thing you want to ask me?" Oh please don't be about my squeaky audition, or the cafeteria with Abigail / Catelyn. "Um, I was um wondering, if you want to go to the Spring Dance with me." WHAT WHAT WHAT DID HE JUST SAY? Billie stands there, mouth open wide, in great shock and can't comprehend what just happened. Conner looks at Billie, shyly, scratching his beautiful luscious hair. "Well, it's my first time to this dance, just thought it'll be nice if we go together." Billie again looks at Conner in disbelief. Me? Really? What should I say? What do I do now? "Ummmm...." Billie resorts to the only thing she knows how to do – run away. She runs as fast as her legs would let her, her heart is beating fast but she can't tell whether it is from Conner's ask or from the running. "Billie!" she can hear Conner calling her from behind but she is definitely not stopping.

Do It Again, Play It Again

Billie gets home. Her mother is already there. She is sitting at the dining room table, with a bottle of Vodka. Drunk again, obviously. "Oh hi Billie." Her mother doesn't even raise her head to look at Billie. "I'm sorry that I'm such a horrible mother. I'm a horrible human

康納和比莉一起走回家。兩人隨意聊起學校的事、電影與籃球，不知怎的，忽然陷入一陣沉默。比莉想起了什麼，好奇問道：「嗯，所以……你剛剛說有問題要問我，是什麼呢？」比莉心中暗自思忖，拜託拜託，別再兜回那個醜態百出的試奏會話題了吧。還有，拜託也別提起學校餐廳遇到艾碧愷與柯特琳的那件尷尬事。「嗯，我在……我在想說，不曉得妳想不想和我一起去參加『春天舞會』。」什麼！什麼！他剛剛說什麼？簡直是晴天霹靂！比莉停下腳步，詫異得張嘴結舌，甚至一度懷疑自己是否聽錯了，她滿頭霧水，不明所以。康納羞怯地看著比莉，有點難為情地抓抓自己一頭好看的頭髮。「嗯，我第一次參加這個舞會，我只是想，如果我們一起去應該會很好玩吧。」比莉盯著康納看，一臉困惑與不解。我？真的？我該怎麼回答？我現在該怎麼回應呢？「哦……嗯……」一旦慌亂無措時，比莉唯一最擅長的一招，便是三十六計，走為上策——逃離。她二話不說，拔腿就跑，拼命跑，一顆心跟著加速猛跳，但比莉分不清自己的心跳是來自快跑或康納的邀約。「比莉！」她聽見康納在後邊叫她，但她說什麼也不肯停下腳步。

being. No guys like me, I'm never going to get a happy ending in life. Sorry that you are involved in my mess." She sobs as she chugs down another glass of Vodka. Drunk and pathetic, another one of her usual vicious cycle, probably got dumped by her new boyfriend. Billie walks over to her mother, not sure to offer words of comfort or to confirm that yes, she is a horrible mother. She stares at her mother's messy hairdo from the back for a while, tries to reach out to her shoulder, but eventually holds back her arms. "Um... I'm just gonna take the trash out." Billie collects trash from the apartment and takes it to the complex trash chute.

She hears one of the distant neighbor practicing piano. The tune is played over and over again. "Practice, that's what you should do." Cameron's words ring in her head. Practice huh. She goes back to her room, picks up the saxophone. She starts with a simple scale. She plays the scale 12 times. Then she plays Heart and Soul in D flat major. She plays it 5 times, a little squeaky at first, but she powers through. She tries a new song, Home Sweet Home, and tries it in A minor. A little rusty, it's a song that she hasn't played in a long time, she needs to go through a few times. She plays maybe 10 times. Her lips are chapped from practice, and her cheeks and

重拾練習，重新演繹

比莉回到家。媽媽也在家，手不離伏特加酒，坐在餐桌上。唉，不必多說，又喝醉了。「哦，比莉，」隨口一句問候，連頭都沒有抬起來。「我很對不起妳，我真是個很糟糕的媽媽。我無藥可救，爛人一個。沒有男人喜歡我，我想我永遠也別想有個幸福的人生了。對不起啦，比莉，把妳也拉進我的悲慘人生。」媽媽一邊啜泣，一邊仰頭再灌下一杯伏特加。醉酒、自憐、自責，比莉已經習慣了媽媽周而復始的負面循環；或許又被新男友拋棄了。比莉走向媽媽身邊，不確定自己到底該安慰，或肯定她的人生確實悲慘。沒錯，她真是個糟糕的媽媽。比莉近距離凝視媽媽披頭散髮與憔悴的身形，她遲疑了一會兒，想要伸手拍拍媽媽的肩膀，但不知怎的，原想安撫的手卻又縮回來。「嗯……我去倒垃圾。」比莉把屋內垃圾收拾好，拿到外面的社區垃圾槽。

經過鄰居家，她聽見有人在練琴。同樣幾個音，不斷反覆練彈。「練習，是妳應該做的事。」卡麥龍的話又在腦中響起。練習啊！比莉返回自己臥室，把薩克斯風拿起來。先從簡單的音階開始練，來來回回練了十二次。然後，她開始吹奏那首《身體與靈魂，降D大調》。比莉吹了五次，一開始出現幾次錯音的嘎吱聲，但她堅持不懈，

tongues are a little sore. But it feels good that she can play that song now. "Billie.... That sounds really nice." Her mother whispers outside her door.

"Ding!" Her phone lights up. Starr is on the screen, "Hi Billie, there is a new video from your friends! Would you like to watch?" Billie picks up the phone. It's a video from Jake Khan. She clicks "Yes" on the app.

Jake was walking out of the gymnasium. The bully duo blocked his way, the taller had a piece of paper in his hand. "Is this the note that you're looking for? It says, Dear Conner, I've been an admirer for a very long time. Ooooh ooooh ooooh! I can't imagine how Conner would feel after seeing this note." The shorter one followed on, "It'll be even better if we post it on our school bulletin board! Everybody's going to know that Jake is a boy-lover!" The tall one continued, "Conner Sutherland's got a boy-lover! This is going to be soooo good! Captain of the basketball team or not, he's got a boy-lover admirer!" Jake looked furious, he clinched his fist tight.

Cameron walked up. "Hey, what's going on? You guys leave him alone." The bullies stepped back from Jake, still mocking. "We found this note in your boy-loving teammate's backpack. He is in LOVE with

持續練習。比莉想試試看一首全新的曲目：《甜蜜的家庭》，她試著以A小調來吹奏。她太久沒練這首曲子了，所以一開始吹得生疏、不流暢，她還需要多練幾回。比莉練了大概十次，嘴唇都乾裂了，連續用力的雙頰與舌頭也有點酸疼。然而，能重新演繹這首曲子，還是讓比莉心曠神怡。「比莉啊……妳吹得真好，很好聽啊。」媽媽在房門外輕聲低喃。

「叮」！手機亮了起來，星兒又出現螢幕上。「嗨，比莉，妳的好友上傳新影片哦！妳想看看嗎？」比莉把手機拿起來。那是傑克的影片。比莉點開連結，準備觀賞。

影片中，傑克走出體育館。流氓雙人組擋住他的去路，高個兒手上握著一張紙，刻意提高聲調：「這是不是你一直在找的紙條？嗯，內容是這樣的——親愛的康納，我已經仰慕你好久了。哎喲！我無法想像康納看到這封信的感受欸。」另一個矮子加碼恐嚇：「我想如果把這封信貼在學校的佈告欄上應該會更勁爆哦！那每個人都知道傑克愛男生囉！」高個兒繼續冷嘲熱諷：「喲，康納有男生仰慕者呢！真是超級棒啊！管他是不是籃球隊隊長，有男生仰慕才最厲害呢！」傑克怒不可抑，憤怒地緊握拳頭。

卡麥龍走上來。「嘿，什麼事啊？你們兩個放他走。」混混雙人組往後退，口裡還念念有詞，不停地揶揄

Conner, and we can't wait to go tell everybody." The tall one snickered and looked at Jake with an evil smile. Jake lowered his head as he sulked with embarrassment and anguish, fist still tightly clinched.

Cameron gave a stern look at all three, and walked up to the bullies. "I'm going to give you a win-win scenario. Let me offer a small amount of token of appreciation, to buy back that piece of paper, you guys keep this shut. How does that sound?" The bullies looked at each other, smiled, nodded, and the tall one speaks up. "100 dollars. No less. This Friday, hand over at the auditorium." "It's got to be next Friday. I need a little time for that much amount. Also, in the alley behind the school not auditorium, nobody can know about this." "Deal. In the meantime, we keep this piece of paper." Cameron, who is 6 feet tall, reached out and grabbed that piece of note out of the tall bully's hand, and immediately tore it up in pieces. "You have my words. I'm the co-captain of the team, my words are worth more than this piece of paper." The tall bully was upset, but Cameron is a lot taller than both of them so he had to let it go. "Your words. Next Friday in the alley after school. Otherwise we are going to tell everybody."

And both left the hallway. Cameron picked up his

嘲笑。「我們在你這個愛男生的隊員背包裡，找到這封情書。他愛上康納哦，我們實在迫不及待要告訴全世界這好消息呢。」高個兒對著傑克不懷好意地竊笑。傑克低著頭，極力壓抑難以言喻的尷尬與怒氣，依舊緊握雙拳。

卡麥龍冷靜而嚴肅地看著眼前三個人，走向那兩個流氓。「我想開啟一個雙贏的局面。這樣吧，讓我來付一筆錢，跟你們買回這封信，你們兩個人就得遵守交易條件，把嘴巴關緊，不可以洩露任何消息，如何？」流氓雙人組面面相覷，詭計得逞，連忙點頭說好。於是，高個兒出價，「一百塊，不二價。本週五付錢，在體育館面交。」「不行，得延到下週五。我需要一些時間來準備這筆錢。哦，還有，面交地點改一下，不要在體育館，放學後在學校後巷，不可以有人知道這件事。」「行！成交！這封信暫時由我們保管。」身高183公分的卡麥龍，一把將那封信從高個兒手中搶過來，二話不說，當場將信件撕成碎片。「我卡麥龍一言九鼎，我是球隊副隊長，絕不食言！我說的話比那張紙更有價值。」高個兒顯然氣急敗壞，但卡麥龍的身型遠比他們高大魁梧，眼見情勢不利，兩人只好作罷。「好，我們相信你說到做到。下禮拜五，放學後，巷口。不然的話，我們就把這個祕密告訴全校。」

兩個流氓這才走開。卡麥龍拿起背包也準備離開現

backpack and started walking away, when Jake yelled towards Cameron. "Just because you are the co-captain of the team doesn't mean that you need to protect me. I could have dealt with this myself. I don't care if everybody knows." Cameron looked at Jake coldly and said, "We can't have distractions in this critical time. You are going to focus and help us win the championship. I'll make sure they don't say anything." And walked away.

Billie closes the app and lies in bed, thinking about that video. Cameron is going to pay off the bullies to keep them quiet, that is such an arrogant behavior. Very characteristic of Cameron, always trying too hard to act like the grown up. I can't believe he yelled at me today! Practice, he said. Oh I'm practicing, you egotistic fake grown up! Despite his effort and great basketball skills, he is still just the co-captain to Conner. Ohhhhh Conner. He asked me to the Spring Dance. But Tianna is in love with Conner. Tianna would be heartbroken to see me and Conner at the Dance. Or maybe she doesn't care anymore, she's busy hanging out with Abigail. So I should say yes to Conner. But… for some reason I'm still thinking about how arrogant Cameron is. What's wrong with me?

場，傑克叫住他。「就算你是球隊副隊長，不代表需要保護我。我自己可以處理。我才不管大家知不知道這件事。」卡麥龍冷眼看一眼傑克，然後說：「在這個關鍵時刻，我不能容忍任何事情來分散你打球的專注力。你要全神貫注，全力以赴，幫助大家贏得錦標賽。我會確保這兩個流氓閉嘴。」說罷，頭也不回地走開。

比莉關上程式，躺在床上，思緒都在那段影片上。卡麥龍想付錢解決流氓的勒索，好傲慢的強勢作風。嗯，典型卡麥龍的人格特質，總是想方設法讓自己看起來像個大人。哦，說到這裡，我真不敢相信他今天對我大吼大叫的，要我「練習啊」！好啦，我這不就練習了嗎！你這個自以為是的假大人！儘管他煞費苦心又球技高超，他也不過是康納的助手副隊長嘛。哦……康納。他竟然開口邀請我一起參加「春天舞會」欸！嗯，但恬娜愛康納。如果讓恬娜看到我和康納一起出席舞會，她鐵定會傷心欲絕吧。哦，也或許恬娜早已不介意了，說不定她和艾碧愷在一起，忙得不亦樂乎呢。所以，我該答應康納的，可是……不曉得為什麼，我卻念念不忘卡麥龍的盛氣凌人。我到底怎麼搞的？

What A Girl Wants?

Next morning, Billie gets to school early. I need to ask Cameron about Jake's video, or something. I just need to talk to him. She heads for the gate to wait for Cameron. Surprisingly Cameron is already there at the gate. He spots Billie and walks up. "... Hi..." Cameron and Billie both say exactly at the same time, equally awkwardly. Then they look at each other and burst out laughing. "You go first," Billie says. Cameron scratches his head awkwardly, "Um, yesterday.... I didn't mean to yell at you. Hope you know that." Billie smiles, also responds awkwardly. "I - I know that. No worries." Cameron breaks into a smile, as they walk together into school. "So, what did our fearless captain Conner talk to you about yesterday?" Cameron asks casually. Billie blushes but doesn't answer. "I actually want to talk to you about something else. Room 203 at lunch?"

Room 203. This time Cameron gets here before Billie. He is sitting on a desk, smiling at Billie tenderly as she walks in. Billie's heart skips a beat seeing his smile. "Hi Cameron." Billie senses a warm soft tone in her own voice. Cameron responds with an equally tender tone. "How can I help you this time, Miss Squeaky? You didn't post anything last night." Billie's heart melts hearing

少女情懷，是詩非詩

隔天早上，比莉比平時更早到校。她心想，我需要問問卡麥龍有關傑克的影片或其他問題；總之，我就是需要找他講個話。她直接到校門口等卡麥龍。出乎預料，卡麥龍早已在校門口了。他似乎也在等比莉，一見她便眉開眼笑地走向她。「嗯，嗨……」卡麥龍和比莉幾乎同時開口打招呼，不知為何，兩人有點不自在。四目交投後，頓時笑出聲來。「你先說吧。」比莉讓卡麥龍先表達。卡麥龍有些難為情地搔著頭皮解釋：「嗯，昨天……我其實不是故意要對妳吼。我希望妳能諒解，不要放在心上。」比莉也不好意思答道：「我……我知道啦，沒事沒事。」卡麥龍釋懷了，笑逐顏開，兩人並肩走進校園。「啊，我們勇猛的康納隊長昨天跟妳說些什麼啊？」卡麥龍隨口探問。比莉滿臉漲紅，但笑不語，岔開話題：「我其實想要跟你說另一件事。午休時間，203教室，如何？」

203教室。這一次，卡麥龍比比莉早一步到教室。他坐在桌子上，滿面笑容地看著比莉走進來。卡麥龍臉上的笑意讓比莉心跳加速。她故作鎮定：「嗨，卡麥龍。」比莉感覺自己的聲調如此溫暖柔和。卡麥龍也以難得的輕柔聲調回應比莉：「這一次要我怎麼幫妳啊，嘎吱小姐？妳昨晚沒上傳任何東西哦。」卡麥龍的輕聲細語，把比莉一

Cameron speak in such a soft manner. Her palms are a little clammy.

"Ummm. It's not about my video. Well, it's Jake's video that I want to talk about." Cameron's face darkens suddenly. He takes a deep breath and scowls. "I explained to you what had happened. What's there to talk about?" Billie is taken back. She doesn't think Cameron would act so strongly to the subject. And she really doesn't think through what she wants to talk about. "Well – I just thought that Jake might need a different type of help, not the type you offered." Cameron's face darkens further. "There is no other type of help that will benefit him. That is the best for him and the team. Period." Billie is upset with how arrogant Cameron is, and tries to defend her ground. "You can buy them off once or twice, but Jake has to deal with this personal issue his whole life, and maybe it's only fair to help him deal with it in a way that he can manage himself. We're in 21st century now, being gay is not that big of a deal anymore." Cameron stands up and coldly responds, "As the co-captain of the basketball team, I can't risk that. Especially for a potential scandal that involves two of our team members. Is that all you want to talk about? I have other things to do." Billie is furious. Arrogant and stubborn!

顆心都融化了。她的手掌心開始冒汗。

「嗯，這一次不是我的影片。我想跟你問問傑克的影片。」卡麥龍的心情彷彿瞬間從高處跌落谷底，風雲變色。他臉一沉，深呼吸，橫眉怒罵道：「我要告訴妳幾次啊？這有什麼好說的？」比莉不由自主地退縮了。她萬萬沒料到，卡麥龍會對這議題如此反彈與反感。比莉也自知理虧，因為她其實並未認真思索自己到底想聊些什麼。「嗯……我只是想說，或許傑克需要的，不是你提供的這種幫助，而是另一種。」卡麥龍的臉更沉，顯然徹底被激怒了。「沒有其他更好的方法可以讓他全身而退了。我已經想過了，那是對他、也是對球隊最好的解套方法了。就這樣！句點。」面對卡麥龍的傲慢與盛怒，比莉備感沮喪與懊惱，不自覺想為自己抗辯。「你可以用錢收買他們一次、兩次，但這是傑克這輩子都要面對的個人問題，也許，幫助他以最能勝任的方式來處理這個問題，是不是對他比較公平呢？再說啊，這是什麼年代了，都已經21世紀了欸，男同志有什麼好大驚小怪的？」卡麥龍似乎不買單，站起來，淡然回應：「身為球隊副隊長，我承受不起任何閃失。尤其這個醜聞涉及我們球隊的兩個成員。好吧，這就是妳要找我說的嗎？如果沒有其他問題，我還有其他事要做，先走了。」比莉很生氣。傲慢又固執

For a second I thought he was nice! "Yes, I think we are done! Good luck with whatever that you are in a hurry to do!" As Cameron walks away from Billie, Billie bursts out: "Oh yeah and by the way, Conner asked me to go to the Spring Dance with him, that's what we talked about yesterday! Not that you care!" Cameron doesn't even turn his head as he responds, "Good for you. Have fun."and storms out of the room. Why is he such a jerk? Billie's eyes are flooded with tears. She doesn't know why she feels this way, being this upset about this egotistic, narcissistic human being.

Billie goes to bed early after a couple hours of practicing on the saxophone. She is completely drained from the emotional rollercoaster interaction with Cameron, all the high's and low's, is a very tiring new experience. She can use a good night's sleep. Alas, teenage hormones doesn't work that way.... She opens her eyes and it is still dark outside. She looks at her phone. 12:00 AM. Couple minutes before Midnight Moment. Sigh, she can't sleep. This is a funny feeling, since even her big fight with Tianna didn't cause this much distress. Cameron King, a character that she never thought would cross paths, is costing her beauty sleep time. Why is he so arrogant? Why is he so stubborn?

的傢伙！有那麼幾秒的瞬間，我還以為他是個暖男呢！「是的，我們談完了。不管你趕著要去做任何事，祝你好運！」卡麥龍走出去時，比莉不知哪來的念頭，不假思索說道：「哦，對了，順便說一下，康納邀請我和他一起參加『春天舞會』，這就是我們昨晚聊的話題。不過，沒關係，我知道你不在乎！」卡麥龍疾風一般逕自走出教室，頭也不回地留下一句話：「好哦，盡情享受。」這傢伙太不可理喻了！悵然若失的比莉，難過又委屈，眼淚撲簌簌流下。她自己也困惑了，不曉得自己怎麼竟對這不可一世的自戀狂，傷神落淚了！

比莉苦練了幾個小時的薩克斯風，便提早上床準備休息。躺在床上，想起與卡麥龍之間的互動，比莉的情緒，像被攪動的一池春水，波瀾翻騰，心力交瘁。疲憊原可換來一夜好眠，但偏偏青少年的荷爾蒙分泌還真不好搞，徹底擾亂她的睡眠品質。輾轉醒來時，外面仍舊漆黑一片。比莉盯著手機看。半夜12點，「深夜微光」程式再過幾分鐘就會出現，唉，她失眠了。這樣的感覺，有些奇妙，即便和恬娜大翻臉時，也沒有令她如此沮喪消沉。卡麥龍，從來沒想過會出現她心底的這號人物，居然毀了她美好的睡眠時間。他為什麼那麼自以為是、目空一切呢？他為什麼那麼固執呢？比莉輾轉難眠，決定再回頭去看她的

Billie tosses and turns, and decides to just get up and look at her phone. "Hey Billie! So nice to see you!" Starr shows up on the screen. However this time, Starr is pointing to a new button. "Welcome to Midnight Analysis Minute!" What the heck is Midnight Analysis Minute? She clicks on the button.

Her latest video shows up, plays up to when Mrs. Hans offered a second audition and stops. Starr shows up again, explaining the situation. "We realized that your posting is incomplete. Please continue with the posting so we can complete the video." Billie is very confused, I don't understand? What does it mean that the posting is 'incomplete'? Starr displays the white text box with her post, urging her to complete the post. She reads her original post.'

"May 30th, 2019. Catelyn's father used his influence as the city mayor, bribed Mrs. Hans and the school board to decide that only the privileged students in school could be in the school band. Lots of talented students auditioned, such as myself, but none of them was accepted. As it turned out, auditions were held for formality only, the band members were pre-determined behind closed doors. If the real talents cannot be in the band, joining the band is a pure joke. I'm glad that

手機。「嗨，比莉！很開心又看到妳了！」星兒出現螢幕上。但這次有新花樣，星兒指向一個全新的按鍵。「歡迎來到『夜半分析時刻』！」哦！這什麼玩意兒啊？「夜半分析時刻」？比莉好奇點開連結。

她自己最新的影片出現了，螢幕停格在漢斯教練向比莉提出二度試奏會邀約的畫面。星兒又出現了，準備解讀這段情境，進行分析：「我們發現妳上傳的資料其實不夠完整。請持續提供更多資訊，好讓我們可以完整呈現這段影片。」這下，比莉更不解了，她實在摸不著頭緒，「我不明白！我的貼文不夠完整？這是什麼意思呢？」星兒隨即展示了白色框框，裡頭累積了比莉之前寫過的內容，星兒催促她再接再厲，把待續的情節補上。比莉重讀了她原來寫的內容——

「2019年5月30日。柯特琳的爸爸以市長身份與勢力，賄賂漢斯教練與學校董事部，背地裡做出決策，規定只有學校裡的特殊分子才能獲准加入學校樂團。很多擁有音樂天分的學生雖然都報名參加試奏會，我也是其中一員，但我們這些資質甚優的學生，都沒有被選上。回頭檢視，所謂試奏會，不過是一場形同虛設的場子，做做樣子而已，真正的樂團成員早在黑箱運作的過程中，關起門來內定了。如果真正有才華的學生因為沒有後台關係而被阻

I'm not in this lame band. I went to see who's all in the school band. Catelyn was there. They played the school fight song. I fell, they laughed, but Mrs. Hans offered me a second chance audition. I declined."

Hmmm. "Complete the post", huh. Well, let me just add something at the end and see if that "completes" the post. Then Cameron's words ring in her head again: "Just write out exactly what happened." Ugh so annoying, I hate him so much but I'm still thinking of what he said! Billie adds, "I asked Mrs. Hans for a second audition."

And clicks "submit". Starr does a 360 flip on the screen, "Thank you so much! We look forward to completing your video!" and closes the app.

Billie tosses and turns all night long. Conner, Cameron, Jake, Starr keep coming back to her dream-like state all night.

擋於門外，那麼，加入樂團就是徹頭徹尾的一場荒謬劇。我很慶幸自己不是這種爛樂團的成員。我去看看學校樂團的成員到底有誰。柯特琳在那裡。他們演奏學校的加油曲目。我撲倒在地，大家都哄堂大笑，但漢斯教練卻願意給我第二次試奏的機會。但因為我不想成為樂團一員，所以，我拒絕了。」

嗯……，「補充資料讓它更完整」是吧？好，我來看看可以怎麼做。不然，我在最後一段加一些資料，讓整段故事完整落幕，再看看這些情節是否足以「讓故事完整」。不知怎的，卡麥龍的話冷不防又在比莉腦中迴盪：「要據實以告。」哎！煩欸！我明明就恨死他了，怎麼還會一直想起他說過的話啊！真討厭！於是比莉寫下：「我跟漢斯教練要求第二次試奏的機會。」

寫完，按下「送出」。星兒以三百六十度翻轉之姿出現螢幕上。「萬分感激！我們期待繼續完成妳的影片製作！」隨即把應用程式關閉。

比莉就這麼折騰了一晚，半夢半醒之間，康納、卡麥龍、傑克、星兒……輪番上陣出現她的夢中。

第六章
CHAPTER 6

偷窺
Peeking out

After the last class, Billie decides to sneak by the band room. The second audition is tomorrow, she wants to get herself ready mentally. Maybe have a listen to what they're currently playing so she can catch up. Or see if anybody else is still making fun of her behind her back. She has found a secret passage that avoids running into anybody and puts her right at the back door of the band room. It involves climbing through fences and diving through bushes but hey, animosity is worth all the cuts and bruises from the treacherous path. After she starts ascending the last and the tallest fence behind the gym, she hears another person climbing over the fence. Somebody else is taking this treacherous route? Who can that be....

She turns her head, it's Jake Khan. Jake and Billie exchange an awkward look, as they continue the climb. "Hey." "Hi." More awkward silence, interlacing with heavy breathing from both fence climbers. "It's odd, isn't it. This app." Jake finally breaks the silence. "Yeah. It surely is." Billie smiles awkwardly, while pulling herself up the fence one step at a time. Jake is faster and taller than Billie, it takes him about 3 big steps to get to the top of the fence while Billie is still huffing and puffing at the bottom. He reaches out to Billie, signaling her hand so he

最後一節下課後，比莉決定要偷偷溜到樂團教室去。明天就是第二次試奏會了，她想讓自己頭腦清醒，心態上準備好要加入這個樂團。先到樂團聽聽他們正在練習的曲目，往後加入樂團，就可以盡速趕得上大家的進度。也或許，還可以看看是否有人在她背後取笑她。她找到一個祕密通道，可以掩人耳目，讓她隱身在樂團教室的後門。只是，要走到祕密通道，可是一路披荊斬棘啊——先翻過圍牆，潛入草叢，啊，為要深入敵營，這一路的險阻障礙所造成的割傷淤青，都要咬牙忍受，不入虎穴焉得虎子！當她開始爬上運動館後方，那道最高也是最後一堵圍牆時，她忽然聽到另有一人也似乎在翻身爬圍牆。咦，難道有人也發現這條步步維艱的祕密通道？到底是誰啊……？

比莉轉頭一看，啊，是傑克。傑克與比莉冷不防打了個照面，當下兩人尷尬不已，但還是沒有停下「翻山越嶺」的決心與步伐。慌亂中不忘互打招呼：「嘿！」「嗨！」隨即是一陣詭異的靜默，空氣彷彿凝結了，只聽到兩人大口大口的呼吸聲。「這個應用程式很奇怪，對不對？」傑克首先打破僵局，表達他對程式的想法。「是啊，確實！」比莉勉強擠出一絲笑容回應，然後再奮力跨上一步，把身體往上撐起。傑克個子高，動作自然比比莉快而利落，他只需要三個大步就輕鬆抵達圍牆頂端，而比

can pull her up. Billie reluctantly holds his hand, as Jake pulls Billie up to the top.

Billie takes a deep breath as she continues to sweat from the fence climbing. She looks over to Jake, he is just sitting there too, taking a breather before climbing down. Billie feels obligated to express her gratitude to Jake for pulling her up, but the air of awkwardness is making her brain a mush. "Thanks Jake. I do this every day but just didn't sleep well last night. Sleep deprivation, you know how that affects your agility. Seriously, I did this yesterday in less than 10 seconds. Probably could've made it up here without your help." Ugh! Billie Lin! Why can't I just say something normal? She blushes even more and feels even hotter.

Cameron's words ring in her ears again: "stop being so self-centered." Ugh fine. I'll stop talking about myself. Billie takes a deep breath, looks at Jake in the eyes, and tries again. "Um... Jake, thanks for the help. You know, I think you're cool. Don't worry about those bullies. You be you." Gosh I suck at this. You be you? Who says that? Billie really wants to slap herself in the face. Jake squeezes a smile. "Yeah, thanks. You too, keep playing that saxophone. I'll be rooting for you."

OK that isn't too bad, he is smiling and talking.

莉還在底下氣喘吁吁攀爬。傑克把手伸向比莉，暗示她也伸出手來，好讓他可以一把將她往上拉。比莉勉為其難緊抓傑克的手，借力使力，傑克一抓就將比莉拉到圍牆頂。

比莉氣喘如牛，大汗淋漓，再繼續下一步行動前，先趁機吸一口氣。她回望傑克，他也坐著暫歇，準備待會兒要再爬下去。比莉覺得，自己似乎該對傑克剛剛及時伸出援手的善意，表達感謝，但當下的情境有些進退兩難，左顧右盼一番，比莉有些不知所措，思緒打結。硬著頭皮，比莉故作輕鬆地說：「謝謝你啊，傑克。我其實每天都這麼爬的，只是今天狀況不太好，因為我昨晚沒睡好。你也知道啦，睡眠不足很容易影響一個人身手的敏捷。我跟你說哦，我昨天真的在十秒內就翻牆過去了。沒有你的幫忙，我應該也可以做得到。」哎呀！林比莉！為什麼我就不能說點其他比較正常的內容呢？話一說完，她恨不得能重來，這下更難為情了，臉漲得更紅，身體感覺更熱了。

卡麥龍的一番耳提面命又浮現心中：「不要再那麼自我中心了」。啊，好吧！我不再自我炫耀了。比莉深呼吸，抬起頭，專注而誠懇地看著傑克，再給自己一次機會。「嗯……傑克，謝謝你的幫忙。你知道嗎，我常覺得你是個很酷的人。不要擔心那個霸凌威脅的鳥事。你安心自在做自己就好。」哦，媽呀！這種說法真的超彆扭。自

Let's try something a little more normal. Billie puts on her casual face. "So.... Why are you climbing this fence? Where are you going?" Jake winks at Billie. "You know very well why I'm taking this route.... To avoid running into those thugs." Billie smirks and winks back. "And you know very well I'm taking this route so I won't run into any band members here." Billie and Jake look at each other and start laughing.

I Could Share Your Burden Too

Billie feels a little less awkward, knowing that there is a special bond between her and Jake: their embarrassing videos. "Do you get that all the time? Um... I mean, do other people harass you because you like boys?" "Not so much harassing... most people are cool with me being gay. It's not a big deal." Jake's jaw line softens. "I – I just don't want Conner to feel weird. He's a good guy, great captain. I know he likes girls. I – I was just trying to thank him for recruiting me to the basketball team and being a good brother to me." Yeah, Conner is a genuinely nice guy. Everybody likes him. He's not easily embarrassed, because he's only got good intention for everybody. Why didn't I say yes to going to the dance with him? Oops thinking about myself again.

在做自己？這句話是誰說的啦？比莉恨不得賞自己幾個耳光。傑克擠出了一絲善意笑容。「好啊，謝謝妳比莉。妳也是啊，繼續好好吹奏妳的薩克斯風，幫妳加油打氣！」

太好了，可以和傑克談笑風生了，嗯，相談甚歡的氛圍輕鬆不少。現在，讓我們再試試其他更尋常的話題。比莉原來緊繃的心也鬆懈了，於是好奇問道：「所以……你為什麼會爬這道圍牆？你要去哪裡啊？」傑克向比莉眨眨眼，回答：「妳應該很了解我為何選這條路徑吧……不想遇到那些流氓惡棍啊。」比莉恍然大悟，也眨了眨眼，以一種「同路人」的了然心態回應：「你也很了解我走這條路就是不想遇到任何樂團的人。」卸下心防的兩人，坐在圍牆上各自吐露實情，這兩個「同路人」不禁相視而笑。

我也能分憂解勞

比莉覺得輕鬆自在多了，感覺自己和傑克之間彷彿多了一個連結彼此的共同媒介——他們都有難以告人的影片。「你常被霸凌嗎？哦……我是指，會不會有很多人因為你喜歡男生而騷擾你、欺負你？」「騷擾倒是不會……知道我是同志的人，大部分的反應都是稀鬆平常，沒什麼大不了。」傑克如釋重負，表情也跟著舒坦。「我……我只是不希望康納覺得奇怪或不舒服。他是個好人，了不

Focus, Billie, stop thinking about yourself.

Billie has an idea. "You know, Conner is a really nice guy. I don't think he'll feel weird about how much you appreciate him. Maybe you can tell him in person so the bullies can't blackmail you or him anymore." Billie's eyes gleam. I come up with an idea to help Jake Khan! Sooooo proud of me. Jake looks at Billie with gleaming eyes. "That's a good idea, Billie. Thanks." Billie really wants to pat herself on the back as she climbs down the fence grinning. See? I can be caring about other people too. You see that, Cameron King? I'm not as selfish as you thought! Billie continues cutting through the thick bushes towards the backside of the band room. The branches and sharp leaves cut through skin on her arms and legs, but Billie is fearlessly moving with a big smile on her face.

Billie finally reaches the back door of the band room successfully. It is still early, nobody else is there yet. She pops down on the floor with the door half open, and pulls out her phone to browse on TikTok while waiting for everybody to show up. She doesn't even hear when somebody walks into the room. Billie sees a tall dark shadow over her phone, shaped like a person. Oh crap!!!! She looks up, it is Catelyn. She is in a lacey

起的隊長。我知道他喜歡女生。我……其實我只是想要感謝他錄取我加入籃球隊，也謝謝他像個大哥哥一樣照顧我。」沒錯，康納確實是個真誠的好男生，簡直是人見人愛。他不惺惺作態，總是坦蕩蕩而不彆扭，或許因為他對人總是心懷好意。咦，既然如此，我怎麼不爽快答應他一起去舞會呢？哦，不對，我又把焦點放在自己身上了。不行，專注，比莉，不要再只想著自己的事了。

比莉忽然心生一計。「傑克，你知道康納人品真的很好。你如果很欣賞他、很感激他，我不覺得他會感覺奇怪。也許你可以私下直接告訴他，這麼一來，那兩個流氓混混就不會見縫插針，拿這個理由來敲詐你或威脅他。」比莉越說越起勁，雙眸發亮。看吧，我也能出個好主意來幫傑克脫困！真是忍不住要誇獎一下自己。傑克看比莉的眼神，也充滿感激之情。「哦，那真是個好主意啊，比莉！謝謝妳。」比莉一邊爬下圍牆，真恨不得對自己拍肩讚賞一番，我太優秀了！比莉得意地咧嘴而笑。看到嗎？我也可以關心別人的需要。你看到了嗎，卡麥龍先生？你以為我是那種自私自利的人？你錯了！比莉繼續潛入雜草叢生的樹叢裡，朝向樂團後門的目的地前進。粗枝與葉片割傷了比莉的手臂與雙腿，縱使傷痕累累，比莉也不以為意，歡欣鼓舞地勇猛前進。

top and ripped jean, with her long hair flowing freely, and a flute in her hand. Billie feels nervous, awkward, embarrassed, and a lot of resentment. Catelyn Tanner, best friend of Abigail, together they make her life so miserable throughout high school. Pretty, skinny, rich, but also plays the flute beautifully. There is nothing this girl can't do, is there? Life is very, very unfair. Billie wants to be in the band so badly, but that also means she will have to be with Catelyn all the time. She's probably going to tell Mrs. Hans about this. She will make sure I can't get in the band.

Say something, Billie. Or do something.... I probably look like an idiot with my mouth wide open. As all these perplexing thoughts gushes through Billie's head, her eyes, nose, the corner of her mouth, all starts twitching together. If you don't know better, you'd think Billie is suffering a stroke. Catelyn looks at Billie casually. "Hi, Billie." Shit. Think of something, Billie. "Uh, hiya, Catelyn. I'm just here to.... um you know.... so I can...." Billie freezes with cold sweat on her face. This is going to be bad no matter what I say. She is going to tell everybody about this. I'll be banned from the band room forever. Farewell, my social life. Billie cannot stop her face from twitching, and she is drawing blank

費盡千辛萬苦，比莉終於成功抵達樂團教室的後門。時間還早，教室內空無一人。她蹲下身，開一點門縫，半掩著；趁四下無人的等候時間，比莉百無聊賴，拿出手機，瀏覽「抖音」頁面。她全神貫注在手機上，渾然不覺已經有人走進教室。比莉低頭看得專注，頃刻間，一個高高的黑影映照在比莉的手機螢幕上，看起來像個人影。不對！比莉心頭一顫，冷不防抬頭一看，糟糕！媽呀！柯特琳就站在她面前。這是什麼情形啊！眼前的柯特琳，花邊上衣配抓破牛仔褲，長髮飄逸，手上拿著長笛，落落大方。這一切來得太突然，比莉驚慌失措，惶惑不安，各種情緒糾結一塊兒，既尷尬又嫉妒不平。柯特琳小姐，艾碧愷的閨蜜，兩人聯手把我林比莉的高中生涯搞得灰頭土臉。這位小姐漂亮、纖瘦、家裡有錢，而且才華洋溢，長笛一把罩；天啊，她有什麼不會的嗎？簡直得天獨厚！人生真是超級不公平，不公平！比莉朝思暮想，就是想要加入樂團，但那也意味著她得要長時間和柯特琳在一起。完蛋了。這下可好。柯特琳會去和漢斯教練告狀吧。她一定會百般阻撓，讓我進不了樂團。

林比莉，妳發什麼呆啊！說些什麼吧，或至少有些行動吧。比莉的思緒糾結成一團亂麻，她的雙眼、鼻子和嘴角開始不由自主地顫抖。若是個不明究理的外人看了，

on any explanation. Catelyn looks at Billie for another second, and casually shrugs. "Good luck with your second audition. Mrs. Hans is right, we could use a good saxophone player." Catelyn turns her head and walks back to her chair to clean her flute. Billie just sits there with her mouth wide open from the initial shock. Huh? What just happened? I'm still alive? What did she just say? Good luck with the second audition? How did she know about that? Also how did she know about Mrs. Hans' comment about a good saxophone player..... !!! OMG, did she watch my video? DOES CATELYN ALSO HAVE THE APP????

Billie's mind is swirling like crazy as she hides behind the band room door and quietly watches the band practice. I thought the app was for people like me... people who are oppressed by the privileged skinny bitches. Jake has the app because he is gay and probably gets harassed all the time. Cameron has the app because he is egotistic and narcissistic. But Catelyn.... Why does she have the app, how is she underprivileged? She watched my video, MY stupid little video? Why? Oh I really need to talk to somebody about this.... I need to talk to Cameron.... Sigh, I wish I kept my mouth shut and not ended things so ugly with Cameron.

會誤以為她大概中風了。柯特琳一派輕鬆地看著比莉，向她打招呼：「嗨，比莉。」糗大了，林比莉，出個聲嘛。「啊，嗨，柯特琳。我只是在這裡……啊，妳也知道啦……在這裡我才可以……」比莉語無倫次，冷汗直流。不管我說什麼，反正大勢已去，我走投無路了。柯特琳肯定會昭告天下。我大概永遠也別想加入樂團了。再見，我的社交生活，從此無顏見人了。比莉的臉不停地抽搐顫抖，她無法控制自己，惶惶然的忐忑不安，讓她頭腦一片空白而詞窮。柯特琳再看一眼比莉，率性地聳聳肩。「祝妳第二次試奏會一切順利。漢斯教練是對的，我們真的需要一個優秀的薩克斯風樂手。」說完，柯特琳悠然轉身，走向她的位置，埋首擦拭她的長笛。比莉呆坐原處，驚詫得目瞪口呆。她心頭一震，啊？剛剛發生什麼事了？我還活著嗎？她剛剛說啥？祝妳第二次試奏會一切順利？她怎麼知道這件事？等一下，欸，她又怎麼知道漢斯教練對我說的話……我們需要一個優秀的薩克斯風樂手？哦，我的天啊！她是不是看了我的影片啊？不會吧，老天啊，柯特琳是不是也有那個應用程式啊？

比莉躲在門後，安靜地窺探樂團練習，錯綜複雜的思緒，剪不斷理還亂。我以為，那個應用程式是為了像我這種人量身定制的……就是被那些既得利益者如紙片惡女欺

Trying To Bury The Hatchet

She slowly walks towards the gym, still thinking about how she can possibly talk to Cameron about this. Basketball team is still practicing hard. She can hear the sneakers squeaking on the gym floor as the team runs through the court. There's Conner. There's Jake. And… Cameron. In the far end of the gym, she also sees Tianna. She is standing in the corner against the wall, staring at Conner. Tianna. She loves Conner, although she completely denies it. Billie smirks and thinks about how much she misses hanging out with Tianna. We've been best friends since kindergarten. We did everything together. But now, she's doing this project with stupid Abigail instead of me. What does Abigail know about her literature program for the kids? I should've been the one helping Ti-ti, not Abigail.

Tianna sees Billie looking at her, waves her hand awkwardly and continues to look at Conner. Billie turns her eyes to Conner. Conner. Captain of the basketball team. Warm, tall, genuinely nice to everybody and does not have a shred of ego or evilness. I don't know why he asked ME to the dance, when he could've had any girl in school. But what did I do? I ran away. Sigh. I really should do better than running away.

麼的對象。傑克有那個程式，因為他是同志，他可能也經常飽受騷擾。卡麥龍也有，那是因為他自以為是，自傲又自戀。可是，柯特琳……她為什麼也有那個程式呢？她怎麼會是弱勢者呢？不會吧，難道她看了我的影片？我那愚蠢至極、醜態百出的影片？為什麼？哦！天呀！我真需要找個人談談……我需要和卡麥龍談談……唉，有點懊惱，我上次為什麼不閉嘴呢？真不該和卡麥龍鬧得不歡而散。

冰釋前嫌，和好如初

比莉放慢腳步，若有所思地走向體育館；她暗自思忖，該如何開口和卡麥龍提起這件事呢？籃球隊正賣力練習。兩派人馬在球場上奮力廝殺，球鞋摩擦地板的聲音，陣陣傳進耳中。看到康納了，還有傑克。還有……卡麥龍。比莉也看到恬娜，在遠遠的角落。恬娜背靠牆，對康納行注目禮。恬娜，是的，她愛康納，雖然嘴裡不承認。比莉苦笑，想起這段時間和恬娜的疏離，心有感慨，她多想念兩人膩在一起的那些日子。她們可是從幼稚園就認識的閨蜜啊，兩人之間無所不談，什麼事都一起做。但現在，她不找我，卻和那愚不可及的艾碧愷一起完成她的企劃案。艾碧愷懂什麼？她怎麼知道恬娜為小朋友設計的文學課程啊？我才是幫恬恬的最佳人選，而不是艾碧愷。

Conner sees Billie looking at him as he defends against Cameron. He awkwardly turns his head to avoid eye contact, as Cameron swiftly dribbles the ball around him and aims for the hoop. Swoosh. A beautiful 3-pointer. Oh wow that's a nice shot! Yay Cameron! Billie quietly cheers for Cameron as he continues to command the court. Cameron. Cameron. Egotistic and stubborn. Calls me names and accuses me of being self-centered. Yet I can't get my mind off him. I practiced saxophone with his voice in my head. I talked to Jake with his image in my mind. Heck I even edited that app thinking about what he said. What the heck is going on with me?

Cameron also notices Billie. He slows down and stares at her for about 2 seconds. His lips move, as if he is saying something. Billie's heart stops. It is the longest, slowest 2 seconds in the history of humankind, Cameron is moving in ultra-slow motion in her eyes. Then he speeds back up and shoots another beautiful 3-pointer. The coach blows the whistle. "All right everybody, great practice today! Keep up the good work, championship next week! Cameron, I need to talk to you." Cameron looks at Billie one more time before he heads over to the coach. Well, so much for trying to talk to Cameron.

Billie walks out of the gym and sees Tianna also

球場另一頭的恬娜，與比莉遙遙相望，彷彿祕密被看穿般，難為情地向比莉揮手致意，隨即再繼續緊盯著康納的一舉一動。比莉也把視線轉向康納。康納。籃球隊隊長。玉樹臨風，高帥又溫暖，待人真誠，溫良恭儉讓。一個條件那麼優的男生，我實在搞不懂他為何會選上我和他一起參加舞會，他實在可以邀請其他女生啊。不過，話說回來，我怎麼反應呢？我居然一溜煙跑掉了。唉，我真是不識抬舉，我其實可以找一個比逃跑更好的回應方式。

球場上，康納正防堵卡麥龍的進攻，一抬眼正好發現比莉也正盯著他看。康納尷尬地避開比莉的眼神，這一分神，卡麥龍見機不可失，身手矯健地運球繞過康納，瞄準籃框，投球。唰，進球。漂亮的三分球。哇！好球！耶！卡麥龍讚！夜郎自大又固執己見的傢伙！愛罵我還不忘批評我自私自利。最糟糕的是，我又對他念念不忘！我練習薩克斯風時，滿腦子都是他的聲音。我跟傑克説話時，滿心都是他的身影。天啊，就連編輯與修訂應用程式的當下，也是想著他的一言一語。我到底是怎麼了啊？

卡麥龍也注意到比莉了。他刻意放慢腳步，盯著比莉凝視了兩秒。卡麥龍嘴唇微動，彷彿在説些什麼。比莉的心跳，瞬間戛然而止。那兩秒的四目交投，是人類史上最漫長、最綿延深情的兩秒鐘，卡麥龍那一望，在比莉心中

walking out. Billie presses her lips together, reminds herself one more time: Ti-ti needs my help on that project, and walks towards Tianna. "Hi Ti-ti." She tries to smile as naturally as possible. "H-Hi, Billie. How have you been?" Tianna fakes a smile. "You know, same old same old. How's the literature project coming along?" "Oh, it's been pretty busy, but a lot of fun. I'm super excited to be helping these underprivileged kids to learn how to read. Feel like I'm running out of time though, since the first event is coming up." Tianna carefully avoids talking about Abigail and glances at Billie with the corner of her eyes. Billie forces a smile on her face. I need to help her. This is Ti-ti asking for help. I still hate Abigail, but Ti-ti is my best friend. "Hey.... So do you still need help with the poster?" Billie murmurs, hoping that she doesn't sound too desperate. Tianna's eyes light up with a huge smile. "I do! I do! Oh Billie thank you!" as she hugs Billie. The twosome chats about the project, giggling and laughing as they walk home together. The awesome duo is back in session!

Later that evening, Billie reaches for her phone and opens the app. Let's check out my completed video! I wonder how they "completed" my video? "Hi Billie! Are you ready to complete your post?" Starr asks cheerfully.

彷彿定格成永恆的超級慢動作。一轉眼，卡麥龍又卯足了勁，再來一顆三分球。教練吹起口哨。完美落幕。「好啦，今天就到這裡，今天大家都練得很好！不要鬆懈，為了下禮拜的比賽，大家要保持最佳狀態！卡麥龍，我有話要和你談談。」卡麥龍先回頭看一眼比莉，再走向教練。好吧，看來，想和卡麥龍說個話還真不容易。

比莉逕自離開體育館，看到恬娜也走出來，兩人不期而遇。比莉緊抿雙唇，不忘再度自我提醒：恬恬的這個計畫需要我的協助。於是，她走向恬娜。「嗨，恬恬。」比莉竭盡所能讓自己的笑容看起來自然些。「嗨，比莉。妳最近好嗎？」恬娜笑得有些不自在。比莉回答：「哦，你知道的嘛，老樣子。哦對了，妳那個文學課程的計畫，進行得如何了？」「啊，最近真的好忙，但還蠻有趣的。我一想到可以用這些教材來幫助弱勢孩子學習閱讀，就覺得非常興奮。最近忙得有些分身乏術，因為第一場活動就快到了。」恬娜小心翼翼地避免提起艾碧愷，一邊以眼角掃視與觀察比莉的反應。比莉強顏歡笑。心想，我需要幫助她。恬恬已經發出求助訊號了。是的，我還是很討厭艾碧愷，但恬恬是我最好的朋友。「嘿……嗯，妳還需要我協助妳設計海報嗎？」比莉小聲探問，免得讓自己聽起來過於急切。恬娜一聽，開心得雙眼炯炯發亮，以最大的笑容

Billie frowns. Huh? Didn't I complete that last night? She clicks on her latest video. Exactly the same, the video ends with her face zoomed in. I thought I added another paragraph in the post last night? What happened to that part? Billie clicks everywhere within the app, but she keeps getting error messages that her action is invalid because the video is incomplete.

"Oh C'mon! What do you mean by video incomplete? You're the one making the video, what do you want me to do?" Billie yells at Starr but Starr just keeps saying 'Please complete your post!'. Frustrated and running out of ideas, Billie throws the phone away, picks up the saxophone and plays every song she's ever known to let off steam. Tomorrow is the second audition. I need to practice. I'll deal with the stupid app tomorrow.

來回答：「需要需要！哦，比莉！太謝謝妳了。」說罷忍不住往前緊緊抱住比莉。冰釋前嫌的兩人，興致勃勃地繞著課程計畫，越談越起勁，走回家的路上，兩人一路咯咯大笑，聊個沒完沒了。終於和好如初了！

當天稍晚，比莉拿起手機，開啟應用程式。來看看我已經完成的影片！我很好奇他們會如何「製作完成」我的影片？「嗨，比莉！準備好完成妳的貼文嗎？」星兒開心詢問。比莉眉頭深鎖。什麼？我昨晚不是已經都寫完了嗎？她點開最近的影片。和之前的一模一樣，最後一幕，依舊停格在她臉部表情的特寫鏡頭。奇怪了，我以為我昨晚已經增加一段敍述了，不是嗎？那一段文字有什麼問題嗎？比莉嘗試在程式的各個角度點閱，但換來的卻是「訊息錯誤」的「無效」反應，因為她的影片還不完整。

「哦，拜託！什麼意思啊，什麼叫影片不完整啊？你是負責製作影片的人欸，你還要求我提供什麼腳本啊？莫名其妙！」比莉對著螢幕裡的星兒怒罵，但星兒不厭其煩地重複：「請您完成上傳資料！」比莉把手機丟開一旁，摸不著頭緒又百般挫折。算了。她拿起薩克斯風，把她會吹的每一首歌，都吹奏一遍，藉此發洩滿腹牢騷與情緒。明天就是第二次試奏會了。我需要好好練習。好吧，明天再來處理那笨蛋程式好了。

第七章
CHAPTER 7

艱鉅大挑戰
A Formidable Challenge

Next morning. Billie is having a hard time getting up. She practiced till really late, and forgot that she had a project due so she stayed up trying to finish the project. "Billie! C'mon, we're going to be late!" A familiar calling from Tianna comes through the window. Billie smiles, gets dressed, and dashes downstairs. The awesome duo is back in session! As she gleefully greets Tianna outside, she hits a sudden brake on her cheerful expression. ABIGAIL! Is standing next to Tianna. Billie hesitates at the door, wondering how she should react. I thought Ti-ti and I are back to being BFF again, what is Abigail doing here?

Tianna senses Billie's hesitation and attempts to break the ice: "Billie, you know Abigail is also helping with my project. I told her that you'd be helping out with the poster, so she wants to talk to you about it." Abigail steps forward towards Billie and talks in her usual bitchy tone. "Hi Billie. Glad to hear that you're helping out on this project. Look, you are very behind, you need to get caught up on the project status. You need to be aligned with what my vision of the poster should look like." Billie takes a step back. She hasn't decided if she should talk, or cry, or yell, or run like hell. She just doesn't deal very well under pressure. She is not mentally prepared to

隔天早上。比莉費了好大一番力氣，才爬起床。她昨晚練習到深夜，才猛然驚覺有一份期限已到的作業要完成，不得不挑燈夜戰，趕工完成。「比莉！快點！我們快遲到了！」熟悉的呼喚聲從窗外傳入，恬娜已經在樓下催促了。比莉笑逐顏開，換好衣服便趕緊衝到樓下去。比莉腳步輕盈，心情愉悅，為這段「破鏡重圓」的情誼而備感欣慰。恬娜站在外面等候，比莉開心打招呼，但她的笑顏瞬間凝結在空氣中。天啊！艾碧愷！她就站在恬娜身邊。站在門口的比莉猶豫了片刻，一時之間不知該如何反應。我以為……我以為恬恬和我已經和好，回到過去「一輩子好閨蜜」的關係了，這個艾碧愷，她幹嘛在這裡啊？

恬娜感受到比莉的遲疑，她試著打破陷入冰點的僵局：「比莉，妳知道艾碧愷也在協助我們的課程嗎？我已經告訴她妳會幫忙處理海報的設計，所以，艾碧愷想和妳討論一下細節。」艾碧愷走向比莉，以她一貫的惡女聲調說道：「嗨，比莉。很高興聽到妳可以和我們一起投入這個計畫。妳之前沒有參與我們的討論，所以有些進度妳沒有跟上，現在呢，妳得趕上我們的工作節奏。妳要設計的海報，得要配合我的想法，我們的方向要一致。」比莉倒抽一口氣。她有些不知所措，面對突如其來的一連串要求，她進退維谷，到底該如何回應——平靜回答、大聲哭

be "aligned" with Abigail at all.

Her palms are getting sweaty and she's looking at Tianna with confusion and frustration. Abigail rolls her eyes to Billie's inability to respond. "Billie Lin. We need to be able to work together if you want to work on this project. We're meeting after school in the craft room, be there or be square." Then she grabs Tianna's arms. "Tianna, let's go. I told you she's not useful." And starts walking away. Tianna looks back at Billie as she walks away with Abigail. Billie feels like crying, cursing, pulling her hair out while running away. But she just stands there staring at Tianna walk away with Abigail.

The rest of the day, Billie just feels really crappy. She thought her friendship with Tianna has been mended, they can be best friends again. But Tianna brought Abigail along and Billie was just not willing to deal with her. After the last class, is her second audition with the band. She drags herself to the band room. She's not feeling confident anymore, her mind is completely occupied from this morning's incident, and maybe tryout for the band is not the best idea at this moment. My life is sucking again. Abigail is ruining my life all over. Hasn't she screwed me so many times already? Why me? She sulks as she stands outside of the band

喊、怒罵咆哮或頭也不回地跑開？比莉向來不擅於面對排山倒海的壓力。她還沒有心理準備要和艾碧愷「方向一致」。

比莉的手掌出汗，她一臉困惑與挫折地轉頭看著恬娜。面對比莉的沉默與無力回應，艾碧愷翻了個白眼，繼續下指導棋：「林比莉。如果妳想參與這項計畫，那我們得要卯起來一起合作。今天放學後在工藝教室開會。就這樣，不見不散！」艾碧愷說完，便拖著恬娜的手亟欲離開。「走吧走吧，我早跟妳說過了，她沒辦法啦。」恬娜被艾碧愷拖著走，頻頻回頭看著比莉。比莉好想不顧一切，放聲大哭、開口怒嗆，然後再拉扯自己的頭髮逃離現場。但現實裡的她，卻如此脆弱無力，只能站在原處看著恬娜跟著艾碧愷的腳步，漸行漸遠。

那一天，比莉的心情糟透了，成天鬱鬱寡歡。她一度以為自己與恬娜的友情已經修復、和好如初了，她們可以重拾一直以來的閨蜜情誼。但恬娜竟然把艾碧愷帶在身邊來見她，難道恬娜不了解嗎？比莉就是不想和艾碧愷有任何瓜葛，她們勢不兩立嘛。最後一堂課，是比莉的第二次試奏會，她要和學校樂團一起配合。她有些意興闌珊，拖拖拉拉，終於來到樂團教室。她原來的一點自信，已蕩然無存，整個心思都陷入當天早晨發生的事而膠著鬱悶，或

room. "OK, Billie Lin! Let's see what you've got." Mrs. Hans waves Billie in.

Fight, Flight Or Freeze

A few band members, along with Mrs. Hans, sit around Billie as she pulls out her saxophone and assembles together. Catelyn is in the audience as well. Billie is jittery and her heart is pumping hard. What if I suck again? Oh who cares, I have no talent. I don't care if I can't get in. There is no point in this audition. Billie is inclined to sabotage her second audition by just walking away. She nervously looks around the room. Mrs. Hans is stern, her legs crossed. Catelyn is coldly smiling and the room is filled with anticipation. Billie takes a deep breath, fingers trembling. Maybe this is a good time to run away. She surveys the room one more time, looking for a quick exit.

What's that? She notices somebody holding up a sign against the band room window. "DON'T SQUEAK, MISS SQUEAKY", it says. A familiar face peeks behind the sign. Cameron! He looks at Billie and gives her a thumbs up. Billie's mouth curves as she tries not to chuckle. All of a sudden, a strong boost of confidence and takes over Billie: I want to be in the band. I'm

許，這個時機點，不適合與樂團配合試奏。我怎麼又覺得自己走投無路了呢？唉，一塌糊塗！艾碧愷毀了我的一生。又是她！她到底要陰魂不散地毀我幾次人生啊？為什麼是我？比莉站在樂團教室外，自顧自地發悶氣。「好吧，林比莉！接下來輪到妳囉！」漢斯教練揮揮手，示意要比莉進來。

戰勝逃避的念頭

幾位樂團成員與漢斯教練圍著比莉坐，比莉拿出薩克斯風組裝，手指放好，準備就緒。柯特琳也在觀眾群中。比莉心跳加速，千頭萬緒揪著她越來越緊張的心。萬一我又搞砸了呢？唉，算了吧，我本來就差人一等，沒有天分！管他呢，進不了樂團也沒什麼大不了。我看這種試奏會也沒什麼意思。不知道哪來的念頭，比莉竟想一走了之，親手砸了自己的試奏會。她怯怯地環顧室內。漢斯教練一如以往般嚴肅，雙腿交叉。柯特琳淡然自若，微笑以對，整個教室鴉雀無聲，屏息以待。比莉用力吸一口氣，手指有些顫抖。也許這是三十六計走為上策的大好時機。她再度小心翼翼地巡視室內一遍，尋找一個可以迅速逃離的出口。

啊！那是什麼？比莉驚覺有人在窗戶旁舉起一個紙

talented. I'm going to fight for it. She lifts her head high, looks everybody in the room, and announces loudly: "I will be playing Home Sweet Home by Jason Turner. In the key of A minor."

With more swags of conviction than anybody has ever seen. Gently yet firmly, she blows air and her soul into the mouthpiece. A long, bright first note starts with a vibrant trill that shakes up the whole room. Billie doesn't remember how the rest of the song went: she sees Mrs. Hans's head bobbing, Catelyn's foot tapping, and Cameron's head moving with the beat. This is her best performance ever, she knows. The song ends with a gentle soulful crescendo, and she bows to the audience. The whole room claps.

"Billie, you practiced, it shows. We're going to talk among the band members, and we will let you know. Thank you." Mrs. Hans smiles and shows Billie out of the band room. Billie takes a deep breath of relief and smiles. I'm glad that it went well. Thanks to Cameron..... Cameron! Billie looks around, no Cameron in sight. That guy, he's just sooooo weird! Billie smiles, a strange sensation of pride gushes through her head. She looks at the sky, and walks away with her head high. At this moment Billie is feeling invincible. Her heart is pounding

板，上面寫著斗大的幾個字：「別嘎吱，嘎吱小姐」。一張熟悉的臉在紙板後方出現，卡麥龍！卡麥龍看著比莉，豎起拇指，給她一個讚。比莉忍俊不住而噘嘴，免得笑出聲來。說來奇妙，比莉彷彿被一股力量灌注，頓時萌生強大的自信與企圖心——我要加入樂團。我有才華有潛力，我要奮戰到底。她抬頭挺胸，信心滿滿地環視群眾，鏗鏘有力地宣佈：「我要吹奏的曲目，是傑森透納的《甜蜜家庭》。以A小調演奏。」

比莉綻放了前所未見的舞台魅力與自信。她堅定而溫柔，不疾不徐地，把空氣與靈魂，吹進了薩克斯風裡。悠揚而飽滿的第一個音符，伴隨清脆而流暢的顫音，撼動了整個空間。比莉吹得渾然忘我，她甚至忘了自己如何把曲子吹完，只記得這些畫面：漢斯教練點頭如搗蒜，柯特琳的腳輕拍地板，而卡麥龍的頭，則不由自主地跟著節奏晃動。比莉深知，這是她這輩子最精彩的演出。這首曲子在悠然而深情的漸強高潮中，結束了。比莉對群眾一鞠躬，下台。全場掌聲如雷。

「比莉，妳的表現證明妳確實用心練習。我們會和樂團成員開會討論，然後再通知妳結果。謝謝妳。」漢斯教練笑容可掬地讓比莉先行離開。比莉如釋重負，春風滿面地離開。一切進行得那麼順利，真是太開心了。感謝卡麥

strong and steady, strutting like the Navy marching band on Independence Day. Her jaw is tightly locked together, and everything is crystal clear in her vision. I think I can do anything. I'm not afraid of anything. Not even Abigail. Billie looks firmly towards the direction of the craft room.

Abigail! I'm coming for you!

In the craft room, Abigail is yelling at the roomful of volunteers. "No! I told you that the theme for next week's event is 'charity', we are sacrificing our time to help these poor kids read. Now go and pick stories that reflect our spirit of charity!" Tianna sits among the volunteers, working on the pamphlets and notebooks. She quietly says to Abigail, "Abigail, shouldn't the theme be more about encouraging the kids to read? Charity doesn't seem right...." Abigail looks at Tianna with a condescending look. "Tianna, you gotta trust me on this. There are way too many ungrateful kids out there. They need to learn about appreciation. Now everybody get to work! Chop chop!" She pulls out her phone and starts texting.

龍……卡麥龍！比莉如夢初醒般，急著回頭尋找卡麥龍，但遍尋不著他的身影。那傢伙，就是那麼奇怪！不過，回頭看看自己，這份耕耘後的收穫，加上穩操勝券的感覺，是如此踏實而美好。比莉心滿意足，走起路來，宛若國慶大典上三軍儀隊般，昂首闊步，趾高氣揚。她的下巴緊縮，眼神犀利，一切都撥雲見日了。我想，這下沒什麼事難得倒我了。我一無所懼。艾碧愷算什麼？我才不怕她。比莉勇敢而堅定地往工藝教室走去。

艾碧愷！我來了！

工藝教室內，艾碧愷對著一屋子的志工同學大呼小叫。「不是不是！我已經說過了嘛，下禮拜的主題活動是『善行』，因為我們犧牲時間來教導弱勢的孩子們閱讀。現在請你們去挑選適合的故事，這些故事要能反映我們行善的精神！」恬娜坐在一群志工同學中，忙著處理傳單與冊子。她輕聲提醒艾碧愷：「艾碧愷，我們的主題是不是應該更著重在鼓勵孩子多多閱讀？『善行』好像不太對……。」恬娜的主張換來艾碧愷不以為然的神情，艾碧愷的優越感持續發酵：「恬娜，這種事你得相信我。現在有太多不知感恩的小孩，他們需要被教育。他們要學會如何感謝。好啦，就這樣，大家繼續工作。快快快！」艾碧

Standing Up Against Injustice

The room works quietly on the pamphlets. "Bang!" The craft room door opens, and Billie walks into the doorway. Everybody looks up to see who just comes in. Abigail lifts her head from her phone. She raises her eyebrows and purses her lips, "Wow Billie Lin, I honestly did not expect to see you here. Good for you." Billie's heart is beating really fast. Maybe this is a bad idea.... I can't be confronting Abigail. The meanest, the evilest person in the whole school.... She's definitely going to ruin the rest of my life for sure.... She squints, trying not to look at Abigail directly in the eyes while contemplating her next moves. "So what are you standing in the doorway for? Go get started on that poster! I already assigned the theme for the event." Abigail commands Billie in her high pitch voice. Where is the nearest door for me to run away....? Billie looks at the closest door for a quick exit..... this feels familiar. She had the exact same feeling at the band room. She remembers what happened at the band room. "DON'T SQUEAK, MISS SQUEAKY" sign and Cameron. Billie chuckles at the thought of Cameron, and starts laughing.

The room looks at Billie in horror, thinks she goes mad under pressure. Abigail's eyes and nostrils open

愷說罷，拿出手機忙著傳訊息。

氣勢爆表的俠女出場

教室內，大夥兒安靜埋首製作傳單。「啪！」工藝教室的門，應聲而開，比莉大步走進來。大家轉頭看是誰進來了。原來低頭看手機的艾碧愷，也抬起頭探個究竟。艾碧愷橫眉豎眼，撇嘴說道：「哎喲，林比莉啊！我還真不敢奢望在這裡看到妳呢！妳開心就好啊。」比莉又緊張了，感覺自己的一顆心，就快從嘴裡跳出去了。嗯，或許這行不通……我恐怕無法面對艾碧愷。眼前這個女人可是全校最難搞、最邪惡的人……她鐵定會把我整死，讓我身敗名裂，永無翻身之日……比莉轉移目光，試著不直視艾碧愷，同時想著下一步該如何出招。「欸，妳還愣在門口發什麼呆啊？去開始製作妳的海報吧！我已經把主題都設定好了。」艾碧愷以她一慣頤氣指使的高聲調，對比莉發號施令。哪裡是最近的出口……？比莉盯著最接近的一扇門，心裡嘀咕，不如拔腿就跑吧……咦，這種逃避與逃離的思維模式，怎麼那麼熟悉……。啊，剛剛在樂團教室內，如出一轍的念頭也曾浮現。她記得後來在樂團教室內超展開的情節與故事。對啦，記得窗戶旁的紙板標語：「別嘎吱，嘎吱小姐」，還有，卡麥龍。想到卡麥龍，比

wide, and also thinks she has gone psycho. Billie lifts her head, looks at Abigail straight in the eyes, and walks right towards her in big steps. Her confidence is back in full bloom, and she feels invincible again. She faces Abigail, only inches apart from her nose. "Abigail. This is Tianna's project, she should be the one who's deciding the theme. I will support her cause and the project." Then she turns to Tianna. "Tianna. What is the theme for this event?" Tianna stands up shyly, looks at Abigail with a little fear, and looks back at Billie. Billie looks so fearless and righteous, so full of conviction. This is Billie like Tianna's never seen before. Courage is contagious. Tianna smiles and announces: "The theme is knowledge. We want to encourage kids to learn, regardless of their environment." All the volunteers clap, other than Abigail. She is looking furious and fuming.... But at a loss for words with her mouth wide open.

Billie goes back home with a sense of great accomplishment. Great sense of accomplishment usually accompanies with a sensation of hunger. Her mom left her a note. "I'll be a little late, microwave food in the freezer, don't wait up." Billie remembers Cameron's note again. "DON'T SQUEAK". Nope, I will not squeak. No more Miss Squeaky. She looks in the fridge. Hm,

莉忍不住暗自竊笑，越想越好笑，不知哪來一陣豁出去的快意，比莉竟肆無忌憚地大笑起來。

這突如其來又有些不尋常的輕狂舉止，把大家都嚇呆了，大夥兒心想，比莉該不會是壓力過大而瘋癲了吧？一旁的艾碧愷，詫異得目瞪口呆，以為比莉精神錯亂了。只見比莉不慌不忙地抬起頭，直視艾碧愷，大踏步走到她面前。比莉是那麼胸有成竹，一副雄心萬丈的大無畏，她不僅與艾碧愷對峙，而且靠得那麼近，近得幾乎快碰到艾碧愷的鼻子了。她不慌不忙地說：「艾碧愷，這是恬娜的計畫，主題應該由恬娜來決定，我支持她的想法，也支持她的計畫。」然後，比莉悠然轉頭對恬娜說：「恬娜，這一次的活動主題是什麼？」恬娜羞怯地站起來，深怕得罪艾碧愷似的，但卻被比莉堅定的眼神而感動。比莉正義凜然的氣勢，銳不可當。恬娜從來不知道比莉也有如此勇敢的一面。恬娜彷彿也被這股力量感染了，她面帶微笑，大聲宣佈：「主題是『知識』。我們想要鼓勵孩子們，無論環境與條件如何惡劣，都不要放棄追求知識與學習。」所有志工同學拍手叫好，只有艾碧愷除外。她怒火中燒，簡直氣炸了……，卻又張口無言，只能咬牙怒視這一切。

比莉帶著滿滿的成就感回家。高漲的成就通常伴隨強烈的饑餓感。媽媽留了紙條給她：「我會晚點回來，微

some leftover ground beef and dry pasta. I can make something out of this. An hour later, her mom comes home. "Hi Billie honey! Whoa, that smells good.... Are you cooking?" Billie smiles at her mom. "I made us some meatball and spaghetti. Here come sit down, mom." They sit down together at the dining table as Billie helps herself to a big plateful of spaghetti. "Here, mom, let me fill up your plate." Billie reaches for her mother's plate and serves her a hefty serving of spaghetti. "Oh honey, I can't eat that much! I'm not a growing kid like you, this is going to straight to my belly!" Billie and her mom both laugh.

That night, Billie chats with her mother about school, the band, how she fought with Tianna, being asked out by Conner, and her fits and starts friendship with Cameron. Her mother listens, laughs, and smiles as Billie describes her tryouts for the band. It's nice when she's not drunk. "Hey Mom.... Why do you drink so much?" Billie drums up courage to ask her mom. Her mother is stunned by the question. She frowns, her mouth twitches, and her eyes well up. "I-I'm so sorry Billie. I-I'm so lonely and scared, I don't know how to deal with my life, and I don't know how to be a good mother. I-I'm trying to hold it together but it's been

波食物在冷凍庫，不必等我。」不知怎的，比莉再度想起卡麥龍的紙板標語——「別嘎吱」。哦不，我當然不再嘎吱。也不再成為嘎吱小姐。比莉打開冰箱，嗯，有些剩下的牛肉與義大利麵。我想，或許我可以把這些材料處理一下，弄點不一樣的晚餐。一小時後，媽媽回來了。「嗨，比莉寶貝！哇，好香哦……妳下廚啊？」比莉喜上眉梢。「我煮了一些肉丸和義大利麵當我們的晚餐。來來，媽，妳坐下來啊。」比莉忙著幫自己盛了滿滿一大碗義大利麵，兩人難得一起坐在餐桌準備享用晚餐。「媽，我來幫妳也盛一盤。」比莉為媽媽裝了滿滿一盤。「哦，寶貝，我吃不下那麼多啦！我不像妳，還在發育成長，這些食物會直接堆積到我的大肚腩！」兩人開懷大笑。

那一晚，比莉心情特好，和媽媽聊起了學校和樂團的事，她和恬娜之間的衝突，她被康納邀約參加舞會，還有她和卡麥龍之間微妙的友情。尤其當比莉把試奏會的過程娓娓道來時，媽媽不但聽得入神，也跟著喜笑顏開。只要媽媽清醒不喝醉，該有多好。比莉話鋒一轉，鼓起勇氣問道：「欸，媽……妳為什麼要喝那麼多酒啊？」赫然被女兒這麼一問，媽媽先是驚訝，然後眉頭深鎖，嘴上囁嚅著哽咽說道：「我……我很抱歉，比莉。我……我很孤單，也很害怕，我不曉得該怎麼去面對我的人生，我也不知道

hard for me. I-I'll be better, I promise." She holds Billie's hands as tears roll down her cheeks. Billie fights back her tears. We all need to fight. "Mom, it's okay. I'm trying to be better too. We'll both work on it." As they hug each other for a very long time.

Later in the evening, Billie picks up her phone and stares at the app for a long time. That was a very interesting day. I did my second audition, and stood up to Abigail. Cameron.... For some reason I feel invincible when he's around. On the screen, Starr keeps reminding Billie: "Please complete your post!" Billie finally clicks on the "complete post" link. She contemplates for a long time, then writes:

"I practiced saxophone almost every night. I did the second audition. I almost ran away, but I didn't. It was.... The best I've ever felt in a long time. Thank you Cameron."

Billie clicks on "submit" button, and doesn't even wait for Starr before she turns off the phone and goes to sleep. This is also the best night's sleep she's had in a very, very long time.

該如何當一個好媽媽。我……我也試著要振作起來，但好難。我……我答應妳，我會越來越好。」媽媽忽有所感地緊抓著女兒的手，淚流滿面。比莉忍著奪眶而出的淚水，是的，我們都要勇於奮戰。「媽，沒關係。我們都一起努力，成為更好的自己。我們一起加油。」母女倆緊緊擁抱，久久不能自己。

那一晚上床前，比莉把手機拿出來，盯著熟悉的應用程式，若有所思。真是高潮迭起的一天啊。我完成了第二次試奏會，與艾碧愷對質。卡麥龍……不知道為什麼，只要他在，我便感覺精力充沛，勇氣十足。手機螢幕上，星兒不厭其煩地提醒比莉：「請完成貼文再上傳！」比莉點開「完成貼文」的連結，沉思良久，然後開始撰寫：

「我幾乎每一晚都苦練薩克斯風。我完成了第二次試奏會。我差點兒就緊張到想一跑了之，逃避挑戰，但最終我戰勝了心中的恐懼。那是……那是一種好久不曾有過、如此踏實而美好的經驗。謝謝你，卡麥龍。」

比莉按下「送出」鍵，還沒等到星兒出現報訊，比莉隨手把手機關了，上床睡覺。今晚，也是她很久不曾有過的好眠夜。

第八章
CHAPTER 8

未完成
Incompleteness

"Ding!" Billie is awakened by her phone. It is only 6:00 AM. She reaches for her phone in bed, wondering who is messaging her this early in the morning. "Hi Billie! We finally finished your video; thought you'd like to take a look!" It is Starr. This early in the morning, really? Billie reluctantly clicks on the app.

The video starts with Billie assembling her saxophone in the band room. She looked nervous. Her eyes were twitching and constantly looking around the band room. Then, her eyes fixated on something on the far window of the band room. She smiled, with an aura of steadiness, announces the song choice, and started with a beautiful trill note. The rest of the song was perfectly executed. She bowed, the room clapped. She walked out of the band room, and ran towards the craft room. After Abigail's hostile greeting in the room, her eyes again fixated on the far window, smirked, and walked towards Abigail with a commanding attitude. She helped Tianna re-establish her project theme, and the video ends with Abigail's mouth wide open.

Billie almost can't believe her eyes. The video captured so many intricate details that she forgot herself in the midst of the heat during the audition as well as in the craft room. Starr comes back on the screen.

「叮」！比莉被手機鈴聲吵醒。清晨六點整。躺在床上，伸手把手機拿過來，比莉心裡狐疑，會是誰那麼大清早給她傳訊息。「嗨，比莉！我們終於把妳的影片製作完成了；也許妳會想要先睹為快！」原來是星兒來報信。那麼早啊？真的嗎？比莉半信半疑地開啟應用程式。

影片開始播放。比莉在樂團教室內拿著薩克斯風，準備就緒。她的神色有些慌張。她雙眼掃射室內，頻頻環顧教室周遭。然後，她兩眼好似發現了什麼，定睛於遠方窗戶的方向。原來緊繃的神情，逐漸舒展開來，她嫣然一笑，轉瞬間，不知哪來的力量，使比莉恢復鎮定與從容，清楚報告演奏的曲目之後，比莉便開始悠然吹出悅耳的音調。她全神貫注地吹奏，完美呈現整首曲子。下台一鞠躬，掌聲四起。她走出樂團教室，奔向工藝教室。面對艾碧愷不懷好意的問候，比莉的雙眼再度聚焦於遠方的窗戶，彷彿那一凝神注視，隨即便賦予她滿滿能量，比莉炯炯有神，得意地笑著走向艾碧愷，以大將之風面對艾碧愷。比莉協助恬娜重新設定她的計畫主題，影片最後的畫面，停格在艾碧愷瞠目咋舌的吃驚表情。

這些影片內容，實在教比莉太難以置信了。其中許多微妙的情感轉折，與錯綜複雜的心境，尤其發生在試奏會與工藝教室內那些高潮迭起的情節，連當事人的比莉都

"Congratulations Billie! You did it, you completed your post!" as he shoots up fireworks in the app background. "You have finally figured out the AI behind this app! You see, everything you do or post in your life, should have a beginning, middle and an ending. Once you start something, you need to follow through for completion. Your story was incomplete because you didn't follow through." "Would you like to watch another sample of a completed video from your friends?"

The small video screen rolls. It is Cameron's posting.

The thugs met up with Cameron in the back alley behind the school. The tall thug asked, "Hey co-captain. Hope you brought your money." The short one smiled slyly, "You don't want your precious secret to be out in the public during this critical time, I'm sure." Cameron smiled at both of them. "I actually have something even better for all of us." And he waved his hand, signaling for somebody. Jake Khan walked up. The bully duo was a little surprised and anguish but tried to keep their upper hand on the situation. "Hey you lover boy. Does your captain know that you are in love with him? Hehe." Jake also smiled. "Oh yeah, he does. He can tell you in person." Jake also waved his arms. Conner walked up.

不記得的細節，影片製作都有精準掌握到。星兒又回到螢幕。「恭喜比莉！妳做到了，大功告成了！」一邊在螢幕背景燃放煙花，以示慶賀。「妳終於理解隱藏在應用程式背後的人工智慧！是這樣的，妳生活中所做、所貼上的每一件事，都應該有起承轉合，然後是結局。一旦妳開始了某個故事，妳就需要堅持與追蹤下去，直到妳最終完成，才算結束。妳之前因為沒有追蹤與交待後續進展，所以妳的故事一直完成不了。」「妳想不想再觀賞另一部妳朋友已經完成的影片？」

網頁跳出另一支影片。那是卡麥龍的貼文。

混混雙人組在校園後巷與卡麥龍見面。高個兒問道：「嘿，副隊長。我希望你說到做到，錢帶了吧？」矮個兒則似笑非笑地威脅：「我相信你一定不想讓這個不可告人的祕密在這麼關鍵的時刻曝光吧！」卡麥龍有備而來，談笑自若：「我其實為大家準備了一個更棒的安排！」說罷他揮手示意，像在召喚某人出場。傑克出現了。混混雙人組大吃一驚，表情有些扭曲，但仍強作鎮定，窮追猛打。「嘿，親愛的小男同志。你的隊長知不知道你愛上他啦？嘻嘻嘻！」傑克不為所動，從容淡定笑答：「對呀，隊長都知道了呢！他還可以親口告訴你們哦。」傑克揮揮手。這回輪到康納走出來。康納咧嘴而笑，有意無意地詢問兩

He smiled wide and asked the duo: "I heard you have something you want to tell me? I'm all ears."

The duo's lips quivered as they slowly walked backwards. The short one immediately sold out: "Its.... It's all HIS idea. I honestly have nothing to do with this." And started running away. The tall bully saw that he was alone against the three tall basketball team members, broke out a nervous smile, trembled as he says: "N-Nah, we were just joking around. We-we don't have any interesting secret. Oh, somebody's calling me, I gotta go! Have a nice day!" and also turned and ran away.

The three looked at each other and laughed. Conner wrapped his arms around Jake's shoulders: "Jake, you can tell me anything. You're like my little brother. Don't ever hesitate next time and cause all these nonsense." Jake looked at Conner and Cameron, took a deep breath, "Sorry about all these. I just didn't know how you guys were going to react to all these. Conner, thanks for being my brother. Cameron, thanks for trying to protect me." Conner also reached out to Cameron with his other arm, "Cameron.... Take care of Jake and others in the team after I'm gone, will you? They look up to you." Cameron smiled quietly and responded, "I will. As a friend, not as a parent from now on. Now let's get back to practice."

位小混混：「我聽說你想告訴我一些事？我洗耳恭聽。」

混混雙人組眼看苗頭不對，本能地後退，嚇得嘴唇發顫，不知所措。其中矮個兒識時務，當機立斷，不惜自保而背叛同黨：「這些⋯⋯這些都是他的餿主意。不關我的事，真的跟我沒關係。」撇清立場後，二話不說，拔腿就跑。高個兒猛然意識到自己已被三個身強力壯的籃球健將包圍，根本寡不敵眾，眼見大勢已去，他低聲下氣地自我緩頰，連聲音都顫抖：「哎喲⋯⋯我們只是開開玩笑而已啦。我們⋯⋯我們其實也沒什麼大不了的祕密。啊，有人在叫我，我得先走一步！祝你們有個美好的一天啊！」話還沒說完便轉身開溜。

三個男生面面相覷，相視而笑。康納把手臂搭上傑克的肩膀，「傑克，你可以放心告訴我任何事。你就像我的小弟一樣，以後不需要猶豫不決或對我隱瞞什麼，省心省事，就不必造成這些困擾。」傑克吸一口氣，對著康納與卡麥龍鄭重表達歉意與謝意：「我為這些事跟你們道歉。我真的毫無頭緒，完全不曉得你們會有什麼樣的反應。康納，謝謝你願意成為我的大哥哥。卡麥龍，謝謝你努力想要保護我。」康納把另一隻手臂伸向卡麥龍，「卡麥龍，我離開之後，答應我好好照顧傑克和球隊的其他隊員，好嗎？靠你囉！」卡麥龍淺淺一笑，回答：「當然。不過，

And then all walked away.

End The Story With Action

Billie smiles as the app closes itself. She's feeling a sense of accomplishment… a very odd feeling for Billie. She's been running away from taking responsibility for anything in her life, and for the first time, she is sowing the seeds to change the narrative of her story. She is creating and writing endings, instead of running away from them. Then she thinks about a few more events in her life. They still need to be completed. She stares out of the window as she contemplates on how to create the endings to those. Tianna's voice breaks up her train of thoughts. "Billie! You up yet? We're late for school!" "Coming!" She jumps up and dashes towards the door.

On the way to school, Tianna can't stop praising how great Billie was in the craft room yesterday. "Billie, you are like a changed person! I can't believe you stood up to Abigail! Oh, this is going to be great, the kids are going to be so excited about this event!" Billie is happy that she and Tianna are best friends again. But… she knows she needs to complete this story. It's a story of her and Tianna, the best friends since kindergarten, working buddies for a kids' literature project. In the corner of

從今而後，是以朋友身份來關照兄弟們，而不是家長。好啦，走吧，一起去練球吧。」三人的身影漸行漸遠，最終消失於螢幕上。

以行動來寫結局

影片結束後，程式自動關閉時，比莉臉上掛著笑容。一種奇妙而特殊的成就感……湧上比莉心頭。比莉這一生，總是在該承擔責任的時候，想方設法要逃避；而這是第一次，她為自己起了個頭，改寫了自己的故事。她不再選擇逃避或逃離現場，以具體行動重新為自己的故事撰寫別開生面的序幕與結局。這麼一想，其他曾經發生在她身上的故事一幕幕浮現腦海裡。嗯，這些故事都尚未完成，還需要一個完結篇。她凝視窗外，開始思索要如何為這些未完成的待續故事，鋪展什麼樣的結局。恬娜的聲音打斷了比莉的沉思。「比莉！妳起床沒啊？我們快遲到啦！」「來啦來啦！」比莉應聲一躍而起，急忙開門下樓。

走往學校途中，恬娜不停地連連誇讚比莉前一天在工藝教室的「豐功偉業」，對比莉的見義勇為，嘖嘖稱奇。「比莉，妳簡直是脫胎換骨欸！我到現在都還不敢相信妳居然像個俠女一樣挺身而出反對艾碧愷！哦！真的太棒了，接下來的活動，孩子們一定會很興奮、很期待！」對

her eyes, Billie spots Conner. Billie's eyes sparkle. Aha! There's my missing ending of this story!

"Hey Ti-ti, give me one minute, I gotta talk to Conner about something real quick." Tianna is surprised and also disappointed. "Um.... Sure, I – I'll just wait here." Billie knows Tianna wants to talk to Conner, but she's gotta make things right first. I can do this. I'm going to make it right, to complete the story.

"Hi Conner." Billie walks up to Conner. Conner responds awkwardly. "Oh, hi, Billie." He tries to avoid eye contact. "Look, Conner. I am sorry. You asked me to the Spring Dance, I ran away. That was completely not cool and... childish." Billie wrinkles her nose saying those words. It is difficult saying those words, but Billie powers through. I have to do this. I have to make it right. Conner forces a smile. "I-I understand, Billie. It's okay. You don't have to apologize." Billie takes another deep breath and looks at Conner. "The reality is, there is somebody else who would love to go to the dance with you. She is my best friend, and I think you two will have a lot of fun together." Conner looks at Billie with a confused yet pleasantly surprised look. "Really? Who is that?"

"You know Tianna, right? She is smart, pretty, super

比莉而言，最開心的莫過於她和恬娜的關係，再度和好如初。不過……她知道關於這段閨蜜關係，她還有未竟的故事情節要完成。這篇故事是關乎她與恬娜之間，這段從幼稚園便開始萌芽的好友情誼，一路到兩人同心為小朋友規劃文學課程的工作夥伴。走著想著，比莉眼角瞥見康納，頃刻間，比莉好似靈光乍現，兩眼閃爍，啊哈！有了！找到好結局了，這下，我的故事有譜了！

「嘿，恬恬，給我一分鐘，我很快回來，我需要跟康納講一件事。」恬娜有點意外，也有點悵然若失。「嗯……當然，我……我就在這裡等妳。」比莉知道恬娜有多渴望與康納說話，但她無論如何得先做對這件事。我可以的。我一定得做好這件事，才能完成我的故事。

「嗨，康納。」比莉走向康納。康納有些彆扭，「哦，嗨，比莉！」口裡問候，但康納的眼神閃躲，試圖避開與比莉眼神對望。「哦，是這樣的，康納，我想跟你說對不起。你邀請我一起參加『春天舞會』，我竟然跑掉了。那真的很不應該，而且，太幼稚了。」比莉皺著鼻子，不好意思地向康納認錯。她以道歉來消除存在兩人之間的疙瘩，要說出那樣的話，按比莉的個性，格外困難，但她還是逼自己承擔起該負的責任。我必須要這麼做！我要把事情做對！康納擠出笑容回應。「欸，我……我明白

kind and generous. You two have so much in common." Conner blushes. "Tianna? Wow.... I didn't even... wow. How dense of me." Conner scratches his head, while his face turns redder and redder. Billie laughs and has an idea. "Hey, are you interested in volunteering for a youth group reading event?" Conner looks at Billie with a confused look, as Jake walks by. "Hey Billie! Awesome job on your audition!" Billie waves to Jake with a swag. "You too Jake! Love what you did to those two!" They exchange a wink as they part. Conner looks at both of them with an even more confused look.

"Billie Millie!" Billie hears running footsteps towards her. She turns around, it's her dad. "Oh I'm so happy that I caught up with you! Your mother told me you are on your way to school." Her dad gives her a big hug, and also says hi to both Tianna and Conner. He reaches to his jacket pocket, and pulls out a little black velvet bag. "Here. This is for you. For your band tryout. It will bring good luck on all your performances."

Billie opens up the velvet bag. It's a rose gold metal saxophone mouth piece. It has a warm rugged handmade look. On the corner of the piece, she sees a set of carved initials. "BL", it says. Billie looks at her father. "BL.... That's me?" Her father smiles warmly. "It's

的，比莉。沒關係啦，妳不必道歉。」比莉有備而來，早已想好下一步對策。她吸一口氣，直視康納，說道：「我想告訴你，事實上，有另一個人非常渴望和你一起參加舞會。她是我的好朋友，我相信你們倆若一起去，一定會玩得很盡興。」康納百般不解，雖然困惑，但那表情顯然是喜出望外。「真的嗎？是誰啊？」

「你認識恬娜，對嗎？她聰明又漂亮，超級善良而落落大方。你們兩人有好多共同特質。」康納聽得害羞靦腆。「恬娜？哇……我竟然從來沒有……，哇！我實在太魯鈍了。」康納感覺臉紅耳熱，不由自主地抓頭皮。比莉得意地笑，打鐵趁熱，立即提議：「嘿，你有沒有興趣到我們青年社團的閱讀活動來當志工？」這下康納更不解了。傑克剛好經過他們身邊，隨口打招呼：「嘿，比莉！妳的試奏會表現得太棒了！」比莉開心回應傑克的肯定。「你也是啊，傑克！超愛你對流氓雙人組所做的反擊！」兩人交換了個心照不宣的眨眼與微笑。比莉與傑克的打岔與對話，讓康納感覺一切都如此撲朔迷離，霧裡看花。

「比莉米粒啊！」後方傳來亦步亦趨的跑步聲。比莉驚訝回頭尋找這熟悉的呼喚聲。啊，那是爸爸！「哦，我實在太開心能趕上你！妳媽媽告訴我妳在上學途中。」父女久別重逢，爸爸先給比莉一個大擁抱，也問候女兒身邊

Bubbie Louis, the great jazz player in New Orleans. You two have the same initials, so I begged him to sell this to me. From now on, BL is for Billie Lin, the great saxophone player from our local town!" Billie and her dad laugh heartily.

"Hey hold on dad," Billie turns around to Conner and Tianna. "Hey Tianna, Conner wants to help on our project too! You two need to talk!" as she gently pushes Conner towards Tianna. Billie watches Conner and Tianna blushed together as they talk about the project. OK now that story is complete. Billie Lin writes another completed post in life! Billie smiles proudly and turns back to her dad. "Hey dad. You wanna walk me to school?" "Sure thing! I'm all yours, Billie Millie." Billie holds her dad's arm and tells him about the band tryout adventures as they walk together.

的好友恬娜與康納。爸爸把手伸進外套口袋，拿出一個絨布小袋子。「拿好，這是要送妳的。樂團試奏會時可以派上用場。這玩意兒會給妳帶來好運，讓妳所有的演出都成功。」比莉打開絨布小袋子，那是個玫瑰金的金屬薩克斯風吹嘴。它有一種樸實無華的手作感。在吹嘴的另一角，比莉發現歪歪斜斜地刻了幾個英文縮寫字母——「BL」。比莉抬頭看爸爸，「BL……那是我，對嗎？」爸爸笑得溫暖，答道：「那是巴比路易斯，紐奧良偉大的重量級爵士樂手。你們兩人的名字縮寫一樣，所以我才拜託他，求他把這個吹嘴賣給我啊。從今天開始，這個BL就是林比莉了，我們這個小城鎮最傑出的薩克斯風樂手！」比莉和爸爸笑得合不攏嘴。

「爸，你等我一下。」比莉急急轉往身邊的康納與恬娜，「嘿，恬娜，康納也想協助我們的計畫！你們倆需要談談！」比莉邊説邊順勢將康納推向恬娜身旁。兩人漲紅著臉，開始有一搭沒一搭地聊起活動的企劃案。大功告成！現在，這個故事有個好結局了。林比莉又完成人生另一個故事了！比莉心滿意足地笑，回頭問爸爸：「爸，你想陪我走路到學校嗎？」「當然啊！悉聽尊便！比莉米粒！」比莉挽著爸爸的手，父女倆邊走邊聽比莉聊起樂團二度試奏會的驚險歷程。

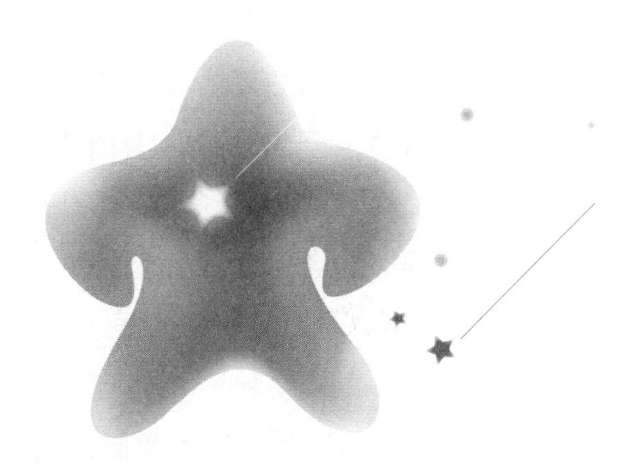

第九章
CHAPTER 9

完成貼文的祕訣
Completion

"Should I wear this jacket, or just the shirt by itself?" Tianna shows Billie her outfit choices. "I really want to wear this jacket that has our school logo on it, but I think Conner likes this shirt on me." Tianna says with a huge smile on her face. "Um, I still haven't heard a big 'thank you' for bringing Conner to your event?" Billie teases Tianna. Tianna blushes and pushes Billie on the ground. "Billie! Stop teasing me! Help me with my outfit! Conner's moving to England next week, I really want to leave the best impression. I mean, we're going to video chat and stuff, but it'll be a while before I can see him in person." Billie casually looks at her phone.

Ever since the last time, she has not seen the app on her phone. Sometimes she misses it. Or maybe... she misses bonding with other people over the app. Like Cameron. "Oh crap Ti-ti, we gotta get going! The championship starts in 30 minutes!" Billie jumps up, grabs Tianna's arm, and heads for the door. Tianna reluctantly brings the jacket with her to the championship.

The school stadium is completely packed with students and parents from both schools. Billie is polishing her saxophone, wearing her band uniform, along with all her bandmates getting ready for the

「我該加這件外套嗎？還是單穿上衣？」恬娜拿不定主意，不確定該以什麼風格的衣著打扮出門，希望比莉提供建議。「我真的很想穿這件印上學校校徽的外套，但我想，康納應該會比較喜歡我單穿這件上衣。」恬娜喜滋滋地自言自語。「欸，我怎麼還沒聽到妳正式跟我說『謝謝』啊？我把康納帶到妳的場子呢！」比莉故意調侃恬娜，向她邀功。恬娜羞澀得漲紅著臉，知道比莉是跟她鬧著玩，尷尬地把她推倒地上。「比莉！妳就別再嘲笑我啦！趕快幫我想想該穿什麼啦！康納下週就要搬去英國了，我真的希望在他心中留下最美好的印象。我的意思是，我們未來當然還可以視訊談話和聯絡，但是，我們要等很久以後，才有機會面對面看到彼此了。」比莉邊聽邊隨意看手機。

自從上回最後一次使用那個應用程式之後，星兒便就此銷聲匿跡，不再出現。有時候，比莉還挺想念那個程式的。或者，嗯，也許……她真正想念的，是與其他人在同一個程式上的連結與共鳴。譬如，卡麥龍。「哦，糟糕，恬恬，我們必須馬上出發！籃球比賽在三十分鐘內就要開始了！」比莉猛然驚覺再不動身就要遲到了，她一躍而起，抓著恬娜的手，奪門而出。恬娜來不及思索，倉促把外套帶著，便跟著衝出門。

halftime show in the locker room. "Has anybody seen Catelyn since this morning? Anybody?" Mrs. Hans dashes into the locker room and asks around nervously. Billie looks around, no sign of Catelyn anywhere. Oh crap, I have a duet solo with Catelyn on the last song.... I'm doomed if she doesn't show up. Billie runs out of the locker room, like a chicken with its head cut off, feverishly looking for Catelyn. She looks in the stadium and spots Abigail playing with her phone, sitting in the front row. Ugh. I need to find Catelyn, Abigail is probably the only person who knows where she is. She reluctantly walks over to Abigail, with a little shake in her legs. "H-Hey Abigail. Have you seen Catelyn?" Abigail looks up from her phone. "Hm. It's you." And looks back at her phone. "Abigail. I need to find Catelyn. You must know where she is." Billie talks louder this time.

Abigail exhales and rolls her eyes. "Probably in the car, being lectured by her mom. They're always like that before any performance." She says all that without looking away from her phone. In the car? What? Billie rushes out to the parking lot. In the middle of the parking lot, she sees the silver Mercedes SUV that belongs to Catelyn's mother. She walks up and sees Catelyn and her mother sitting inside. Her mother seems to be scolding

學校體育館內，兩方隊伍的同學與家長都齊聚一堂，場面熱鬧非凡。比莉忙著擦拭自己的薩克斯風，換上樂團制服，與其他團員在後台的更衣室準備就緒，要在中場休息時演奏。「有沒有人看到柯特琳？有人看到嗎？」漢斯教練緊張地詢問隊員。比莉環顧四周，還真的沒看到柯特琳。啊，糟糕！最後一首曲子有我和柯特琳的雙獨奏……，她若沒有出現我就慘了，我死定了！比莉跑出更衣室，像隻無頭蒼蠅般，心急火燎地到處尋找柯特琳。她在體育館發現艾碧愷在第一排椅子上滑手機。唉！雖然我要找的人是柯特琳，但最有可能知道柯特琳行蹤的人，恐怕只有艾碧愷。好吧，非常時期，也無計可施了，只能硬著頭皮去打探。雖然雙腳有些顫抖，比莉還是鼓足勇氣上前詢問艾碧愷：「嘿，艾碧愷。妳有看到柯特琳嗎？」艾碧愷抬起頭，看了一眼比莉，不以為然地應聲答道：「哦，是妳啊。」然後再低頭看手機。「艾碧愷。我需要找到柯特琳。妳一定知道她人在哪裡。」情急之下的比莉，聲量不自覺更大了。

艾碧愷呼了一口氣，翻了個白眼。「可能還在車上吧，被她媽媽教訓。每一次有什麼演出之前，大概都是這樣的模式。」艾碧愷視線沒離開過手機，說得一派輕鬆，彷彿理所當然。比莉滿頭霧水，在車上？這是什麼狀況？

at Catelyn, and Catelyn is full of tears.

Catelyn Is In Trouble

What's going on? Billie slowly walks up to the car. Catelyn's mother notices Billie walking up and rolls down the window. "No need to get any closer. We'll be done in a minute." And rolls the window back up. Catelyn wipes off her eyes, her mother starts applying makeup on Catelyn's face as she continues to scold her. A minute later, Catelyn walks out of the car, in her band uniform and a fresh beautiful makeup on her face that barely covers her puffy red eyes. She coldly looks at Billie. "It's nothing. Don't make a fuss out of this." Billie frowns. Nothing? You were crying your eyes out. "What's going on? You can tell me. We're band mates." Catelyn looks away as she sniffs. "I told you it's nothing. I don't want to talk about it." And quickly walks towards the stadium. Billie wasn't sure if it was really nothing. She needs Catelyn to be in her usual self, so the band can perform well.

She quickly walks to Catelyn and pulls out her new rose gold saxophone mouthpiece from her pocket. "You know, I'm quite nervous about this performance today, to be honest. My dad gave me this mouthpiece from

比莉十萬火急地衝向停車場。柯特琳的媽媽常開的那台銀色賓士休旅車，就在停車場正中間。她往車子方向走去，果真看到柯特琳和媽媽端坐車內。從車窗望進車內，柯特琳似乎正在被媽媽責備，只見低頭被罵的柯特琳，眼裡噙著淚。

很有事的柯特琳

到底怎麼了？比莉放慢腳步，趨近車子。柯媽媽注意到比莉的身影，搖下車窗。「不必再靠過來了。我們再一分鐘就結束了。」說罷立即把車窗搖上。柯特琳擦拭淚水，柯媽媽一邊幫她補妝，嘴裡卻沒閒著，繼續開罵。一分鐘後，柯特琳下車，身上早已穿好隊服，雖然臉上都化好妝了，卻難以掩飾一雙哭得紅腫的雙眼。她冷眼看一眼比莉，故作鎮定：「這沒什麼大不了的，拜託妳不要小題大作啊。」比莉皺眉質疑，沒什麼？妳剛剛明明在車上哭得稀里嘩啦的。「到底怎麼了？妳可以告訴我呀，我們是樂團的隊友啊。」柯特琳抽了一下鼻子，別過臉去，刻意避重就輕。「我已經告訴妳了，沒事沒事！反正我就是不想講啦。」柯特琳邊說邊加快腳步走向體育館。比莉不確定柯特琳是否有事，但無論如何，她需要柯特琳恢復原來的狀態，唯有這樣，整個樂團才可能好好演出。

Bubbie Louis for good luck. It helps me calm down, so I won't squeak like my first audition. You were there at my first audition.... That was pretty embarrassing, wasn't it?" Catelyn looks at her mouthpiece, then looks at Billie, then chuckles. "Yeah it was pretty bad, your first audition." They look at each other and burst out laughing. Catelyn looks at the sky as she slowly vents, "My mom only accepts perfection from my flute playing. Last night I was pretty tired and my practice was a little off, so she was giving me a hard time this morning." Billie looks confused.

"What? Your flute playing is always perfect." Catelyn smiles. "Thanks, but not in her eyes. I've been playing flute since I was 7, and she is super strict. Sometime she can be pretty mean, saying that my playing is so bad, nobody wants to hear that crap. It hurts, since I practice so hard." Huh..... skinny bitches don't always feel perfect and invincible? Billie cracks a smile, and tries to say something encouraging to Catelyn. Billie thinks of her dad. "You know what my dad always says? He says music is all about making people feel good. You need to feel good about your playing so other people can feel that vibe." Catelyn looks at Billie sternly, and says coldly: "I don't need somebody like you to tell me what to do, Billie

於是，比莉跑向柯特琳身邊，把那全新的玫瑰金吹嘴從口袋裡取出。她說：「柯特琳，妳知道嗎，坦白說啊，我對今天的演出實在有點緊張。我爸爸特別送我這個巴比路易斯的吹嘴，就希望給我帶來好運。這份禮物幫助我平靜下來，我就可以不必重演第一次試奏會的醜態百出。妳當時也在場啊，超級尷尬的，對嗎？」柯特琳瞥一眼比莉的吹嘴，再看看身旁的比莉，認同地輕笑：「對呀，妳第一次試奏會真的蠻慘的。」兩人好似想起了共同的記憶，忍不住相視而笑。柯特琳卸下心防，說：「至於我的長笛演奏呢，我媽媽只能接受我無懈可擊的完美演出。昨晚我有點疲憊，練習品質不太理想，我媽很不滿，唉，所以今早讓我吃盡了苦頭。」比莉百思不解。

「什麼啊？妳的長笛已經吹得很完美了，好嗎！」柯特琳不以為然地苦笑：「謝謝啊，但在她眼中可不是這麼看的。我七歲就開始學長笛，我媽媽是嚴格的虎媽。有時候她會把我批評得一文不值，說什麼……沒有人會想聽我吹這種爛曲子。當我很費力用心練習的時候，聽到這種話，還蠻受傷的。」啊……，紙片惡女原來也會有感覺不完美和脆弱的時候呢！比莉笑著想要說些安撫的話來鼓勵柯特琳。她想起了爸爸。「妳知道我爸爸是怎麼說的嗎？他的論點是，音樂不過就是為了讓人們感覺美好。但是，

Lin. You should focus on getting that solo duet as perfect as possible, try not to drag me down." She quickly walks towards the stadium, leaving Billie behind staring at her back. That skinny bitch. The nerves, what's with that sudden change of attitude? I hate her absolutely!

Back in the locker room, Mrs. Hans gives the band a last-minute pep talk. "Everybody.... Quiet! Hope you all remember the order. Fight song first, marching song next, jazz song to end the show. Keep your formation tight, watch your drum major the whole entire time please. Catelyn and Billie, make sure your duet solo is loud and in sync." "Yes Mrs. Hans!" The whole band replies together.

Outside, the two basketball teams are neck in neck.... Host: 32, Guest: 34. Conner is leading his team the best that he can, while Cameron and Jake are completing many perfect passes and catching loads of rebounds. The guest team shoots another 3-pointer, and it's good.

I Back You With Heart & Soul

The loud horn in the gym signals the first half is over. Score is at 32:37. As the band lines up getting ready to enter the court, Billie can see Conner, Jake and

柯特琳，除非妳自己先感覺美好，否則妳如何能讓聽的人感覺美好呢？」柯特琳忽然板起了面孔，冷漠回應：「林比莉，我不需要像妳這樣的人來告訴我該怎麼做。妳管好自己的事，把待會兒的雙人獨奏吹完美一點，不要拖累我，害了我！」柯特琳疾步往體育館方向走去，把比莉拋在後頭。比莉望其身影，十足紙片惡女，神經兮兮的，不知好歹，這態度說變就變！真的超討厭她的！

回到更衣室，漢斯教練給大家上場前的最後提醒：「大家聽好……，安靜一下。我希望你們記得這些曲目的順序。第一首是加油曲，第二是行軍曲，然後是爵士樂做結束。保持隊形，拜託啊，大家要隨時跟著鼓的節奏前進。柯特琳和比莉，妳們兩人的雙獨奏音量要夠大，節奏要和諧。」「是的，漢斯教練！」全隊齊聲回應。

球場上，兩隊人馬還在廝殺搏鬥中，主場球隊得分32，對手來勢洶洶，得分34，看起來勢均力敵，不分軒輊。康納已盡一切努力，帶領整個球隊，而卡麥龍與傑克也傳出連連好球助攻，掌握許多投球時機，令人刮目相看。才說著呢，對手又準確無誤地投進一個三分球，哇，好球。

Cameron's sweaty and tired faces huddling around their coach. Cameron sees Billie from a distance in her band uniform and gives her a faint smile. Cameron. Thank you all the help you've given me. I wish there was something I can do in return. Drum major whistles, all band members raise their instruments. Billie focuses back on the band duty.

With the drumbeat, the band steadily marches out into the stadium. All students stand up and sing along to the school fight song, as the band transitions to the jazz song ending. Trumpet section starts with a bright upbeat beginning, followed by a three-quarter drum beat, and the drum major points to Catelyn and Billie. Catelyn and Billie slowly march towards the front while playing with the band, and with a flick of the wrist, drum major signals the solo duet between saxophone and flute. Billie and Catelyn look at each other, nod together, start their back-and-forth solo duet. They move together in sync, left and right, back and forth, trilling together with their instruments. The crowd cheers as they end their duet. Catelyn and Billie bow to the audience and march back with the band. "Good job Billie! Good job Catelyn!" Mrs. Hans gives both of them a big hug as the band members all cheer for their performance. Billie smiles

各自全力以赴

哨聲響起，上半場結束了。得分比數是32比37，暫時落後五分。樂團列隊準備進場到正中央時，比莉看到康納、傑克與卡麥龍都氣喘吁吁地汗流滿面，大夥兒略顯疲態，圍著教練聚攏，交頭接耳地說話。卡麥龍遠遠瞥見一身隊服的比莉，給比莉一個迷人笑容，比莉暗自思忖：卡麥龍，謝謝你為我所做的一切。我真希望能給你一些回報。擊鼓的隊伍響起，所有樂團隊員舉起手中樂器。比莉把專注力拉回，全神貫注在演奏上。

隊伍跟著鼓聲節奏，整齊劃一地前進到體育館中。全體學生起立，跟著音樂唱起了加油歌曲，精神昂揚。最後結束前，樂風轉而進入爵士節奏，宏亮的小號聲打起了頭陣，緊接著是四分三切音的擊鼓聲，活潑的節奏首先拉開序幕，指揮引領柯特琳與比莉從隊伍中緩緩走到前頭，兩人邊走邊吹，鼓手一陣連擊，帶出薩克斯風與長笛的雙獨奏。比莉與柯特琳彼此對望，點個頭，一前一後，默契十足地開始吹奏。她們左右、前後地移動，和諧的步伐，搭配悠揚悅耳的顫音，響徹體育館。完美的雙獨奏，群眾報予如雷掌聲。柯特琳與比莉一鞠躬，從容回到隊伍裡。「吹得好，比莉！柯特琳，妳也很棒！」漢斯教練給兩個女生一個大擁抱，整個樂團也為她們出眾的表現歡呼。比

big and looks at her rose gold mouthpiece. Thanks for the good luck charm, Dad.

The second half of the championship continues. Conner is visibly tired as they struggle to get a competitive edge against the guest team. Score at 65:65, with 5 minutes left in the game. The other team shoots a 3-point, Conner jumps with his arm high attempting to block the aim. A player from the other team jumps in front of Conner to block his attempt and lands on top of Conner as they both fall on the floor. Conner screams, the coach asks for a time out, as the team gather around Conner to see if he's okay. The medics comes, and takes Conner out on a stretcher as he cringes and holds his shoulder.

Billie looks over to Tianna, she is in tears full of worry on her face. Coach pulls Cameron to the side, whispers in his ears, then huddles with the rest of the team. When they get back in the court, Cameron assumes Conner's captain position. Cameron! In the captain position! Billie cheers and smiles, standing on her toes so she can see better. The score is at 65:68 with 4 minutes left. Cameron seems to struggle to pass the ball to his team members. Billie is biting her nails as she watches the game on the sideline. I must do something...

莉看著爸爸送的玫瑰金吹嘴，開心不已。老爸，謝謝你的幸運禮物。

下半場籃球賽開始了。面對這場硬仗，雙方隊伍旗鼓相當，康納帶領的主場隊奮力搏鬥，卯足了勁南征北討。最後五分鐘，康納顯然已精疲力竭，兩隊人馬打成平手，65比65。眼看對手瞄準籃框，準備投下三分球之際，康納一躍而起，高舉手臂試圖來個隻手遮天，阻撓進攻。不料，對方一名球員忽然竄出彈跳，擋在康納前方，這一跳雙雙都重摔倒地。一陣劇痛令康納忍不住尖叫，教練立即要求暫停，隊友一擁而上，圍繞康納，關切他的傷勢。康納抓著肩膀呻吟，醫護人員上前將他抬離球場。

比莉看一眼正在觀賽的恬娜，恬娜的臉上淌著淚水，憂心忡忡。教練把卡麥龍拉到一旁，在他耳畔說話，然後，把其他隊員都召聚一起，想是給球隊做最後的戰略佈局與緊急提示。當大夥兒重返球場時，卡麥龍替補了康納的隊長角色。哦！卡麥龍！他臨時被委以重任，擔起了隊長的職分！比莉興奮雀躍而笑不攏嘴，一邊踮起腳尖，想找個更好的視角。最後四分鐘，65比68。卡麥龍猶豫著是否該把球傳給隊友。情勢告急，在球場邊緊盯著球賽的比莉，緊張而焦灼。我得做些什麼……我得做些什麼……啊！有了！她找到一張白紙，和一支麥克黑筆，在紙上寫

I must do something.... Ahhh I've got it!! She pulls out a piece of paper and a black marker, writes something, and clips the paper on her hat then stands closer to the court on a chair. Cameron please see this. Please see this. Look over this way.

Cameron has the ball and slowly dribbles across the court, looking to find a gap among the defense. As he surveys the team formation, he notices Billie standing tall on the sideline with the paper on Billie's head. He chuckles, and breaks into a big smile. He immediately takes a deep breath, dribbles with one hand and points to Jake with the other, passes the ball to Jake. Jake jumps to attempt a dunk while the other team tries to block, but it is fake – Jake casually throws the ball sideways back to Cameron as he shoots a 3-pointer. The crowd cheers.

Figuring Out The Algorithm

67:68, 1 minute left. The guest team has the ball. As their captain slowly dribbles the ball back, Cameron gives Jake a signal with his head. Jake nods, and speeds up to the captain to steal the ball. The captain quickly passes the ball to his teammate, where Cameron is already waiting.... He intercepts the ball, while Jake runs back to home court. Cameron makes a long pass to Jake,

了些字，然後，把紙條夾在自己的帽子上，再蹭身往球場靠近，站在一張椅子上。卡麥龍，拜託拜託，看過來這裡。

場上的卡麥龍，接到傳來的球，跨越中線，緩緩運球前進，想要在層層防守中突圍而出。當他眼觀四方，審視隊友的站位時，他瞥見了球場邊的比莉，還有她頭上無法忽視的那張紙，卡麥龍忍不住暗自發笑。他隨即深吸一口氣，然後，將手中的球傳給傑克。傑克緊抓著球，疾如閃電般躍身投籃，對手衝上前防守，但原來那是傑克的假動作，他聲東擊西，一轉身把球拋給守候另一邊的卡麥龍，只見卡麥龍一接到球便如蛟龍出水，唰，三分球準確無誤地投進籃框。全場歡呼雷動。

找到演算人生的大智慧

67比68，最後倒數計時，只剩一分鐘。發球權掌握對方手中。對方的隊長不疾不徐地運球到他們的進攻場域，卡麥龍對傑克點頭示意。傑克收到指示，衝上前試圖搶下隊長的球。隊長趕緊把球傳給其他隊友，站好戰略位置的卡麥龍，成功攔截下半空中的傳球，千鈞一髮之際，卡麥龍把球用力長傳給已經奮力跑回本場的傑克，傑克一搶到球，便一躍而騰空投球，灌籃得分！哨聲響起，球賽結

and Jake dunks! The crowd stands up in a roar as the horn blows, signaling the end of the game. 69:68. Billie screams and jumps along with her bandmates, hugging everybody in celebration.

After the game is over, Billie packs up her saxophone and changes back to her street clothes in the locker room. "Ding!" it is a text from Tianna. "Conner dislocated his shoulder but doing ok. At the hospital with him. Go home without me." Billie smiles and starts walking home. "Hey Miss Squeaky." A familiar voice. Billie smiles and turns around. Cameron is standing behind Billie, with a gym bag on his shoulder. "Congrats on the championship, captain." Billie teases Cameron. Cameron scratches his head, smiling a little timidly: "Well, not yet technically. Coach told me I'll officially take over next month, after Conner moves to England." Cameron walks together with Billie.

"Hey.... Thanks for the um, note on your hat. You know, it's still there on your hat." He says shyly and points to the hat in Billie's hand. Billie looks at her hat and blushes. "Oh yeah... forgot to take it out." It says "DON'T SQUEAK". "You know... I've never thanked you for your note at my audition." Billie looks seriously at Cameron. "I don't think I could have done all these

束，69比68。群眾早已按捺不住激動的情緒，心潮澎湃，紛紛起立歡呼。比莉與樂團團員興奮得手舞足蹈，大夥兒彼此擁抱慶賀。

球賽結束了。比莉走回更衣室，換回便服後，收起她的薩克斯風。「叮」，手機傳來恬娜的簡訊。「康納的肩膀脫臼，但無大礙。我在醫院陪他。別等我，妳自己先回去。」比莉笑著讀完簡訊，一邊移動腳步，準備回家。「嘿，嘎吱小姐！」好熟悉的聲音。比莉回頭看，笑臉盈盈。卡麥龍站在她身後，肩上背著運動包。「恭喜隊長啊，旗開得勝！」比莉刻意開他玩笑。卡麥龍搔搔頭，笑得有些靦腆：「哎，技術上來說，還沒正式上任啦。不過，教練告訴我，下個月康納搬去英國之後，我就會正式接任當隊長了。」卡麥龍和比莉並肩走著。

「嘿……嗯，謝謝妳剛剛掛在帽子上的紙條。那個……那張紙條還在妳的帽子上哦。」卡麥龍不好意思地指向比莉頭上的帽子。比莉揚眉抬眼看自己的帽子，瞬間面紅耳赤。「啊，對哦……我忘了拿下來。」那紙條上是斗大的三個大字：「別嘎吱」。「欸……，我一直還沒有機會跟你正式道謝，就是試奏會那天你在後面給我舉牌提示。」比莉異常認真地看著卡麥龍。「我想，如果沒有你，我恐怕沒辦法完成這些目標。卡麥龍，謝謝你。」卡

without you, Cameron. Thank you." Cameron responds with a warm smile. "I'm sure you could. I also want to thank you for helping Jake and myself." Billie grins, raises her head to look at the sky. "Too bad we still don't figure out the algorithm behind the app AI. But Starr told me that I finally completed a post so that was some accomplishment." Cameron chuckles, "Ah, you too? Good to know I'm not the only one struggling to complete a post." Cameron and Billie laugh, and gaze at each other. Maybe I can write an ending on this story too.

"Hey Cameron...." "Yes?" "I'm just wondering.... Do you want to go to the Spring Dance with me?" Billie's heart is pounding hard again. Oh shit, what am I doing???? Cameron tilts his head and thinks for a while. Awkward silence. Why did I have to ask him to the dance? Stupid me always ruining things..... Suddenly, a car pulls up in front of Billie and Cameron. A silver Mercedes SUV. Isn't that... Catelyn's car? The car stops, Catelyn casually steps out of the car and walks towards Billie and Cameron with a stern look. Oh crap. She's going to lecture me about that solo duet, for sure.

Catelyn stops in front of Billie, looks at Billie condescendingly as usual. Here it comes. "Billie Lin... we

麥龍以溫暖的笑容來回應比莉。「我很確定妳能做到！對了，我也要感謝妳用心幫助我和傑克。」比莉露齒而笑，抬頭望天。「真可惜，我們到現在還找不到那個應用程式的演算法。不過，星兒告訴我，我的貼文總算大功告成，我感覺還蠻有成就感的。」卡麥龍調侃笑道：「哈，妳也是哦？真高興發現原來不是只有我在掙扎怎麼完成貼文。」卡麥龍和比莉怔怔凝視彼此，兩人因際遇雷同而捧腹大笑。嗯，也許，我也可以來為這段故事寫個結論。

「嘿，卡麥龍……」「是，怎麼了？」「我在想說……你會不會想跟我一起參加『春天舞會』？」話一出口，比莉心跳加速。卡麥龍微傾著頭思考，一陣尷尬的沉默，令人有些不知所措。我幹嘛邀請他去舞會啊？笨死了我，這下嗝屁又搞砸了……。忽然，一輛車毫無預警地停在他們面前。銀色賓士休旅車。咦，那不就是……柯特琳家的車？果然，是柯特琳。她走下車，向比莉與卡麥龍走來，表情嚴肅。哦，糟糕了，她肯定是衝著雙獨奏的演出來教訓我了。

柯特琳在比莉面前駐足，一如以往般，以高高冷冷的姿態，看著比莉。她終於開口說話了。「林比莉……，我們今天一起合作的演出，很棒。其實，妳的表現真的了不起。謝謝妳在表演前對我說的那番話，很奇妙，那段對話

had a great show. Actually, you had a great performance. Thanks for our little conversation before the show, surprisingly it helped calm my nerves. I'd appreciate if you keep this as our little secret. Looking forward to playing more duets with you." Catelyn says all these with not a shred of expression on her face, and immediately turns away, gets in the car and takes off. Cameron looks at Billie very confusedly, and Billie looks at the back of the car with her mouth wide open.

"You.... Her.... Wanna explain what just happened?" Cameron finally breaks the silence. Billie takes a deep breath and looks at Cameron, slowly nodding with an enlightened smile. Catelyn and the app! I've got it, I've got it! I finally understand why Catelyn has the app! "I don't know if I can explain well.... To be honest. But I think I learned one thing: everybody feels insecure at times. Even the most perfect people feel pressured to be the perfect themselves. Maybe that is the algorithm behind the Midnight Moment AI all along. It's okay to be insecure, everybody does, more importantly we have to follow through and complete what we have started. Whether it's my dream to be in a band, or to be a good friend to Tianna and you. We can't let insecurity be in the way of completing what's important to us." Billie

幫助我平靜下來，讓我不再那麼緊張。如果妳能把今天看到的一切都當成我們之間的祕密，那我真的會非常感激。很期待未來還有很多機會和妳一起雙獨奏。」柯特琳面無表情地一口氣把話說完，然後迫不及待地，轉身上車，比莉還來不及反應，車子轉瞬駛離，留下呆若木雞的比莉與滿頭霧水的卡麥龍。

卡麥龍百般不解地看著比莉，「妳……她……想要解釋一下剛剛到底是怎麼一回事嗎？」卡麥龍忍不住開口詢問。比莉深吸一口氣，看一眼卡麥龍，忽然，好似想通了什麼，比莉從錯愕困惑中，恍然了悟露出微笑。啊哈！我懂了，柯特琳和程式！我終於明白柯特琳怎麼會有那個程式了！「坦白說，我不確定我能不能解釋得清楚……。不過，我倒是認清了一件事——原來每一個人都有缺乏安全感的時候。即便外表看來多麼完美風光的人，都會在追求卓越的過程中，感覺壓力重重。搞不好，這或許就是『深夜微光』這人工智慧程式背後的演算法則。缺乏安全感不是問題的癥結，人人都有缺乏安全感的時候與課題；但更重要的是，我們要持續不放棄，努力去完成起初設定的目標。不管我的夢想是不是加入樂團，或一心想要成為你和恬娜的好朋友；我們不能任由『缺乏安全感』來阻礙我們完成重要的目標。」說完，比莉再深呼吸一口氣，遙望柯

takes another long breath and looks at Catelyn's car in a distance. She tilts her head and blinks with a mysterious gleam in her eyes. Catelyn, hope you can overcome your insecurities and follow through with what's important to you too.

"Miss Squeaky. You are one unpredictable person. And a very good friend of mine." Cameron smiles tenderly looks at Billie as he continues, "The dance.... I hate those social events. They are always designed for non-productive chit-chatting." Billie looks up at Cameron with a slight frown. Cameron hesitates when their eyes cross. He scratches his head with a deep blush on his face, stuttering a little: "B-but... going with you will be a lot of fun." He smiles at Billie embarrassingly. Billie smiles back. "It's a date, then." "It's a date, Billie." Billie and Cameron continue walking, in complete silence but flooded with smiles on both faces.

All of a sudden they hear somebody yelling their names from the back, followed by sound of running footsteps. "Hey Billie Lin! Cameron King! Wait up! I'm so glad to see you both!" Cameron and Billie stop and turn around. It is Erin Lancaster, the freshman nerd. Erin catches up to them, stops to catch her breath while breathing heavily. "Phew.... So glad to see you guys!

特琳的車子離得越來越遠。她偏頭思索，眼中閃爍一絲靈光。柯特琳，希望妳也能克服缺乏安全感的屏障，努力堅持更重要的目標。

「嘎吱小姐。妳真是個令人捉摸不透、不可思議的人。當然，也是我很好的朋友。」卡麥龍讚賞而溫柔地笑，一邊看著比莉繼續說道：「至於舞會……我其實很討厭這一類的社交活動。這些場合到最後，總是離不開一些無聊的聊天打屁。」比莉皺眉盯著卡麥龍看。兩人四目交投時，卡麥龍遲疑了一下；他習慣性地搔搔頭，臉一下又紅了，講起話來結結巴巴：「可……可是，跟妳一起去，應該會很好玩。」卡麥龍羞澀地傻笑。比莉鬆了一口氣，粲然一笑，回答：「那就當做約會囉！」「是的，比莉，是個約會。」比莉與卡麥龍繼續並肩前行，雖然兩人沉默不語，但心花怒放的愜意，盡寫在臉上。

一陣急促追趕的腳步聲與呼喚，打破沉寂。後方有人叫他們的名字。「嘿，林比莉！卡麥龍！等一下！啊，看到你們兩個人實在太好了！」卡麥龍與比莉循著聲音，回頭一探究竟。那是伊琳藍卡斯，高一新生，典型宅女。伊琳邊跑邊呼喚，上氣不接下氣地，把兩人攔下，請教學長姐：「呼……很開心見到你們！是這樣的……我最近在我的手機下載一個應用程式，叫做『深夜微光』。我在裡面

You know, I've just installed this app called Midnight Moment on my phone. Saw both of your videos, big fan! Still trying to figure out how this app works, can't seem to get it to post what I wrote.... Any pointer? Any secret codes that you can share?"

Billie and Cameron look at each other with a mischievous smile.

看到你們的影片欸！我愛死了，被你們圈粉了！只是我還在努力摸索如何使用這個程式，我覺得奇怪，不曉得為什麼我發現自己寫的內文一直貼不上去……你們有什麼建議嗎？是不是有什麼祕訣可以告訴我啊？」

比莉與卡麥龍兩人四目相交，交換了個促狹眼神，啞然失笑。

深夜微光──App的奇幻世界
Midnight Channel for Teenagers

作　　　者／Kelly Kuo
中　　　譯／童貴珊
企 畫 組 稿／林幸惠
校 對 協 力／吳琪齡、湯耀洋

發　行　人／王端正
總　編　輯／王志宏
叢 書 主 編／蔡文村
叢 書 編 輯／何祺婷
美 術 指 導／邱宇陞
美 術 編 輯／金魚

出　版　者／經典雜誌
　　　　　　財團法人慈濟傳播人文志業基金會
地　　　址／112019臺北市北投區立德路2號
電　　　話／02-28989991
劃 撥 帳 號／19924552
戶　　　名／經典雜誌
製 版 印 刷／禹利電子分色有限公司
經　銷　商／聯合發行股份有限公司
地　　　址／231028 新北市新店區寶橋路235巷6弄6號2樓
電　　　話／02-29178022
出 版 日 期／2021年3月初版
定　　　價／新臺幣300元

ISBN 978-986-99938-5-2（平裝）
Printed in Taiwan

國家圖書館出版品預行編目（CIP）資料

深夜微光：App的奇幻世界
= Midnight Channel for Teenagers/
Kelly Kuo作；童貴珊中譯. -- 初版.
-- 臺北市：經典雜誌, 2021.03
224面；15*21公分
ISBN 978-986-99938-5-2（平裝）
863.57　110003047
1.青少年心理 2.青少年成長

小樹系列

Little Trees

小樹系列

Little Trees